Depression

Robert Romanis

MA, MB, BChir (Cantab)

faber and faber

LONDON · BOSTON

First published in 1987
by Faber and Faber Limited
3 Queen Square London WC1N 3AU

Photoset and printed in Great Britain by
Redwood Burn Limited
Trowbridge Wiltshire
All rights reserved

© Robert Romanis 1987

British Library Cataloguing in Publication Data

Romanis, Robert
Depression.
1. Depression, Mental
I. Title
616.85'27   RC537

ISBN 0–571–14674–0

Contents

Acknowledgements

I should like to thank Dr Reginald Kelly and Dr John Pollitt, both of St Thomas's Hospital, for their sympathetic and helpful comments, and suggestions about material, at an early stage of this book; my then secretary, Mrs Prue Seddon, for cheerfully walloping through draft after draft at that stage without benefit of word processor; my wife, who made the final manuscript legible for my present secretary Mrs Gloria Day to type; and finally, I suppose, the British and German Armies which, each in its own way, gave me my first personal experience of depression.

1

What is depression?

Depression is a subject of enormous concern to its sufferers and their families: but so hedged about with silence and embarrassment, so confused in diagnosis and treatment, that it is often difficult for patients to get information and help through the barrier of ignorance and lack of sympathy that surrounds them. This sad situation is all the more distressing because a sense of shame and isolation are themselves symptoms of the illness; and as things tend to be at the moment, the patient is all the more cut off from help. Depression is in fact a fairly clear cut subject and its treatment is effective and by psychiatric standards fairly rapid; and the intention of this book is to demonstrate this to the general public.

We must be clear we are talking about depression as an illness rather than a normal reaction to depressing circumstances. We are all unhappy from time to time, and indeed in some circumstances we should be mad not to be. Bereavement, unemployment, bad housing, an unhappy marriage, the antics of teenaged children or elderly parents, failure at work or at play, personality clashes with other people, any of these may depress us when we experience them. But this depression, though somewhat resembling the illness, goes less deep, is less widespread in its symptoms and affects far less of the sufferer's personality, life and capabilities. Above all, this depression is commensurate with and appropriate to its cause. Many a depressed, that is to say an ill, patient has said to me, 'but I've nothing to be depressed *about*'; which is almost diagnostic as a start. The sort of everyday depression I am writing about in this paragraph bears some sort of relationship to the severity of the misfortune which is its cause; and though it is hard to say what is proportional or commensurate to a bankruptcy or a bereavement, in general this is a type of depression which in its circumstances surprises neither the patient nor his or her friends.

Depression the illness, which from now on will be the only depression under discussion, is frequently or usually quite disproportionate to the apparent and obvious conditions of the patient's life: which has led to the tortuous, probing, detective-story approach of some schools of psychotherapy. It has moreover many diagnostic features which are absent in everyday depression as we shall see; and it is these features, these symptoms which define it as a genuine straightforward illness and not the moral failure that patients feel it to be.

In all cases, diagnosis depends on some uniformity of behaviour of the illness; if pneumonia differed hugely from patient to patient not only could we not diagnose it, it would not be a true classifiable disease entity. Depression in the medical sense shows a quite astonishing uniformity of symptoms between patients, making it firstly a true disease entity and secondly fairly readily and accurately diagnosable. In my experience it is an illness that may be easier to diagnose than acute appendicitis.

So the first point I want to make is that depression is an illness not a moral failure. Secondly, it is not at all uncommon, and no depressed patient need ever feel alone. There are no statistics about depression: only those few patients who are admitted to hospital appear on any records, and for every patient who sees any doctor at all I feel sure there are two or three others too shy, ashamed and confused to approach a doctor. People don't talk about their depressions so no one else knows they are ill: shame of the illness, as we shall see, is one of the symptoms.

Thirdly, it can be treated. We shall discuss this later on and all I shall say here is that treatment of depression is more satisfactory than that of chronic sinusitis, and the great majority of patients are sufficiently recovered to be leading a pretty normal life in about three months. Many indeed are never off work at all. Many of *these* who do not see a doctor wear out weeks and months in the belief that this is not a treatable illness, or that treatment must take many months of psychotherapy.

2

The depressive in society

All this in the previous pages is said to rescue patients, and their families, from the largely mediaeval view of 'mental' illness that is still remarkably prevalent. It has always been regarded as different in kind from 'physical' illness, requiring quite different methods of diagnosis and treatment; and even calling for a different moral approach. Physical illness, it was felt, was outside one's control: what went wrong with the body was not one's fault. Even when the illness or injury was the direct result of the patient's carelessness, folly or downright criminal behaviour, the actual physical consequence was felt to be just bad luck, and the patient the blameless victim of circumstance. When a foolish young man had broken his leg in a traffic accident, or an untrained middle-aged one had injured himself skiing, the actual result of their folly or neglect was treated with the same care and sympathy as if it were heroically sustained in battle.

'Mental' illness on the other hand seemed to have something wanton about it. Because there were no x-rays, physical findings or blood tests (though this last is no longer true), people felt the patient was not *ill* at all. 'Mental' illness was marked by a change in behaviour or attitude, and it was hard for the unsophisticated not to feel that the patient could change back if he really wanted to. Moreover, 'mental' illness involved more of the patient; a broken leg is only my leg, but a sickness of personality is *me*; it was felt that mental illness somehow involved the soul and the patient's whole moral persona.

Hence the curious embarrassment most people usually display in talking about illness such as depression. It is hinted at, alluded to; curiously moral-sounding terms such as a breakdown are used; people never *have* one: they are always on the *verge* of one, with emphasis on the word verge. Even quite kind people say censoriously that their friends 'have problems they can't cope with', a way in which they would never refer to a broken hip, which is a problem nobody can really cope with. And because 'mental' illness seems to involve a patient's whole personality in a way a broken leg doesn't, those who haven't broken their legs merely regard themselves as lucky, while those who haven't had a depression secretly regard themselves as somehow stronger and more responsible than those who have: a point of view, as we shall see, with which the depressed patient is all too willing to agree.

This moral view of mental illness had its opponents quite early; Robert Burton in his *Anatomy of Melancholy* of 1621 was able to regard depression as an observable illness rather than a moral failing; and by the middle of the nineteenth century some doctors were beginning to treat depression on lines broadly comparable with other illnesses. Then the rise of post-Freudian psychoanalysis and in particular its very wide amateur and popular application set the whole process back a hundred years or more with its authority, its use of moral, social and even theological jargon, and its tortuous, detective-puzzle approach. Many people's idea of psychiatric treatment is based on the Hollywood cliché of the man in a white coat putting together a jigsaw puzzle of the patient's past; and this cliché has probably done more harm to the popular understanding of depression than any other.

It has led to the impression that the cause of all mental illness lies in the distant past, and its treatment consists in endlessly dragging up that past until every tiny detail is remembered. Once that point is reached months or years later, and in the case of psychoanalysis a positive storm of emotion has been gone through, the patient is cured. Meanwhile the patient has remained ill all this while and been subjected to an additional series of stresses which he or she can ill afford. A patient may be told that he or she must 'work through' the guilt which is such a feature of the illness: in my view this is as silly and ineffective as telling a patient with pneumonia that he must work through his cough. Similarly, great emphasis may be laid on those problems the patients cannot cope with; and one school of psychotherapy regards depression as a problem-in-living to be solved like other problems (and with the same difficulty); instead of an illness, quite likely caused *by* those problems, but an entity as separate *from* the problem as a broken leg is separate from the rickety flight of steps that may have caused it. All depressed patients are beset with intractable problems: but when the illness is better either the problems are found to be fears and shadows, or the patient sets to work effectively to solve them. In this sense the problems are not *the* problem: the problem is a treatable illness.

As an example, a very intelligent man in his early thirties came to me deeply depressed and with good reason. He was in debt, his company was on the rocks and his marriage was breaking up. He had good insight into his condition and said gloomily, 'I suppose it will take months and months of psychiatric treatment to get me well.' Three months later after the sort of management we shall discuss in this book he was still in debt, his company was still on the rocks and his marriage was still breaking up; but he was working effectively to solve these problems, and solve them he did.

To be fair, to bring mental illness into the same category as physical illness, or rather to wipe out the distinction altogether so that depression and gallbladder disease are simply two examples of organic illness, one needs some knowledge of brain physiology; and this of course Freud and his immediate followers lacked, just as Galileo knew no nuclear physics. But even before brain physiology reached its present imperfect state, there were plenty of examples of mental illness with a wholly organic basis. Various poisons were known to produce temporary psychoses; the other name for rabies, hydrophobia, has a thoroughly psychiatric ring. Influenza, jaundice, childbirth have all for many years been associated with various degrees of depression, and the direct connection has never been doubted.

Subtler and more striking examples could be quoted: in extreme thyroid deficiency, the patient exhibits physical changes, becoming heavy, pale, cold and bloated, and may also become an idiot. In the same way a cretin is the technical term for a child born without a thyroid, who untreated will grow up physically handicapped and mentally deficient. In either case the right dose of thyroid given in time will restore the patient to normal physical and mental health.

Similarly, in a type of anaemia once called pernicious but now more often called Addisonian, the patient may become profoundly disturbed or even psychotic if the level of vitamin B12 in the blood falls below a certain critical level. Here again a sufficient dose of the vitamin will convert an aggressive unco-operative patient, violent in manner if not in action, into a normal pleasant person, rational about treatment and able to make a full recovery.

All this preamble is the process I call de-Freuding, and is intended to show that mental and bodily illnesses are not necessarily as separate as they used to be thought; and that these so-called mental illnesses do not necessarily have a long historical introduction which needs elaborate unravelling before the patient has any hope of recovery. Depression is an organic illness to the same extent that hypothyroid dementia is organic, and responds to similar organic treatment.

It is a stress illness, occurring in people of a certain personality, in which well-known changes occur in the biochemistry of the brainstem (and can be demonstrated or at least inferred from blood tests), and in which an extraordinarily uniform series of symptoms develops. These symptoms are astonishingly similar in a very wide range of apparently different patients; they are similar in patients of different races and cultures, and they run more true to form than those, for instance, of acute appendicitis. It is only by these symptoms that the illness can be recognised, in which of course it is the same as all other illnesses.

The people in whom the illness occurs are themselves of a pretty recognisable personality. Their characteristics include hard working, conscientiousness, some perfectionism, some obsessionalism. They tend to be rather buttoned up and may be poor at expressing their emotions, not least because they respond too well to that belief in the stiff upper lip from which the British think they uniquely suffer. In a sense they are less adaptable than others because they may lack the easy-going pliability that enables people to absorb change and survive it.

People of this temperament are good workers, reliable and responsible, and are often found in positions requiring leadership and decision-making; and where moreover displays of impatience and ill temper have to be avoided and controlled. They are self-punishing people, who take their stresses out on themselves instead of losing their temper or throwing hysterics and taking it out on others. Depressives are very nice people.

3

Stress

It is necessary to digress on the subject of stress. We talk as if stress were invariably a bad thing, a cause of malaise, even perhaps a malaise in itself. This is not strictly so: it is a term borrowed from the engineers by doctors, psychologists, social workers and the 'Worry Industry' in general, and by and large misused. An engineer will tell us that many structures will fall down unless stressed; certain arches are only stable when they are loaded. On the same analogy nobody has ever called pre-stressed concrete particularly fragile stuff.

We swim in stress like a fish in water; it is like the tons of atmosphere that weigh constantly on our skins; and if the stress were totally removed we should probably collapse like an unstable arch. Stress gets us out of bed in the morning, keeps us alert crossing the road, makes us earn a living, gets us to the church on time. In a sense stress was and is the mainspring of evolution; and in this I mean no emotive approval of 'Victorian values'; it is mere physiological fact.

Most people prefer it this way; they would sooner be 5 per cent overworked than 10 per cent underworked; and this will show stress is not in itself bad. When we talk about stress in a bad sense we really mean excess stress, and it is in this sense that I shall normally use the word.

The concept of stress in medicine has been used to construct a sort of 'General Theory' of attack and defence, in infection, trauma or everyday wear and tear. All states of health, whether good or bad, are in this context the result of a balance between assault and defence, whether the assault be a virus, a block of concrete or the annual audit. If the defence

9

withstands the assault, the patient is well, however precariously; if the assault overwhelms the defence, the patient becomes in some sense ill. A feeble assault (a less than deadly microbe, a small block of concrete, an easy annual audit) is easily fended off by the defences; overwhelming assault will defeat any defence. But a feeble defence will go down before a feeble virus and will not need an overwhelming assault.

Thus, though one does not catch a cold from being cold, if I'm in the Underground cold, wet, tired, hungry and very probably worried and fed-up, I shall catch a cold from an anonymous well-wisher who sneezes in my face, in a way I should not catch it if I were fit, warm and cheerful. And the same principle with appropriate variations applies to all the other slings and arrows that the flesh is heir to, whether they are material or moral.

The excess stresses that may lead to depression may be wholly physical, wholly emotional or a mixture of the two. The physical are in fact reasonably familiar: jaundice and influenza are famous for the depression that follows them, and that dreary disease glandular fever is also followed by a very characteristic depression marked particularly by physical lassitude. The milk-borne diseases – the brucelloses (Malta fever, contagious abortion, undulant fever) – equally cause depression, sometimes during rather than after the disease, and getting better as the disease improves. Of the depression of malaria a patient said, 'It's the end of the world, and it's all your fault.'

Apart from acute infections, prolonged debilitating illness may lead to depression, though here it is a little doubtful whether this is a wholly physical stress or whether the emotional stress of a long illness plays a large part. The same can be said of post-partum depression (depression after childbirth): though here the obvious hormonal element is pretty certainly the predominant one, fitting more neatly into our description of physical stress.

Direct physical trauma and the physical shock involved in it can certainly lead to depression, the more so if the patient has been concussed as in a traffic or riding accident. Surgical operations can be followed by depression, and here I believe the anaesthetic is the trigger for the illness rather than the knife. Some heart specialists believe that the use of a heart-lung machine during heart surgery specifically causes depression. Being wounded or blown up in a war or terrorist attack may also lead to depression: but here of course the whole experience is so complex that one cannot separate physical and emotional elements. Finally, certain poisons and drugs can cause depression, either immediately or as part of withdrawal and recovery.

The wholly emotional stresses include bereavement, over-work, emotional shock such as the sudden discovery of terrible news, or any period of frustrated emotion that cannot properly be expressed. Sometimes the stress can be short and sharp; sometimes it may be prolonged over years, and perfectly sustainable until either the limit of endurance is reached or some other and possibly very minor stress is added.

The mixture of physical and emotional is probably the commonest cause found. A woman in her early forties, who had successfully weathered twenty-five years of marriage to a fairly exacting husband, three rowdy sons and the usual stresses of a house and family, had a minor operation and three weeks later went into quite a severe depression of which I believe the ordinary stresses and strains of life were the *cause* and the operation, probably the anaesthetic, the trigger.

The illness may come on during the period of stress. But not infrequently the lifting of the stress is the trigger precipitating the illness. This is the psychological cliché of the soldier who is all right in action but becomes ill ('breaks down' as people say) when he finally comes out of action. There is the example of the widow who has nursed her husband through a distressing illness, or withstood the shock of a sudden bereavement magnificently; and copes splendidly with death and its material aftermath; but becomes ill perhaps weeks later when all the work and bustle are over, and she has time to relax. I shall have more to say about this later when we come to discuss the phenomenon of arousal (p. 61).

4

The mechanism of depression

When this type of excessive stress acts upon that type of personality beyond the capacity of the defence to withstand it, the hypothalamus becomes deficient in carbachol-amines, and thus becomes inefficient.

At this point we have to introduce 'Tiny Tots' Physiology', partly because it is most important for the patient to have some idea of what is going on in his or her brain, and partly to emphasise that we are talking biochemistry, not Freudian guilt complexes. The hypothalamus is a complicated area at the base of the brain (close to the pituitary gland, the so-called master gland of the body) on the one hand representing an old or primitive stage in the brain's development, and on the other to be viewed as a kind of switchboard or relay station between the conscious parts of the brain with which we perceive and know and think (or think we do) and those wholly involuntary activities of the body which we cannot immediately influence by conscious thought. Thus although we call the jump we give when the door slams involuntarily, we can voluntarily imitate it by a direct effort; but we cannot blush or blanch or make our hair stand on end by trying to do it. We have to think the proper thoughts, or perhaps the improper thoughts, and the effects then follow through the intervention of the hypothalamus.

The bodily functions controlled or mediated by the hypothalamus include:

1. *Sleep pattern* – it is normal to sleep by night and wake by

day, to sleep in a series of waves of deep sleep and lighter sleep, to dream regularly, and so on. In or after certain illnesses people may sleep by day and wake by night, or cat-nap at intervals throughout the twenty-four hours; and in depression as we shall see there is a characteristic shift of sleep pattern.

2. *Metabolism* is to some extent under hypothalamic control, affecting appetite, body-weight and body temperature – we all know people who worry themselves thin *or* fat, and few people can have failed to have had the experience of losing all appetite though worry or distress.

3. *Heart rate* may be similarly affected, and nobody needs to be told how the heart may race or thump in emotion – we have all had this experience.

4. *Sexual activity* also may be modified by the hypothalamus, which again is not surprising considering what a fragile affair sexual desire and performance can sometimes be.

All organs get tired in some sense or another, whether it is the heart, the kidney, the brain or the left big toe, and the hypothalamus is no exception. It is a useful but not wholly proved suggestion that under stress (i.e. in excessively fatiguing circumstances) the hypothalamus uses up the hormones and enzymes grouped together as carbachol-amines or mono-amines at a higher rate than normal, so that the supply of hormones to activate those chemical changes inseparable from any physiological activity decreases, and these activities slow down. I have said the hypothalamus becomes inefficient, and its functions shift usually in the direction of underactivity or depression. It may, as we shall see, shift the other way in the direction of overactivity or excitation: though we shall also see that in certain cases such as sleep pattern it is difficult to say which exactly is under- and which is overactivity.

The mechanism of depression

Some people are surprised at the use of the word hormone in this connection; there is a popular misconception that all hormones are sex hormones. But in fact the hormones whose names are more familiar to people than any other are insulin and adrenaline; and most of the hormones, or chemical messengers, of the body have nothing to do with sex. One of the hormones of the mono-amine group that become deficient in depression is noradrenaline; and most depressed patients respond instantly and gratefully to the suggestion that their brain is short of adrenaline.

5

The cardinal symptoms
of depression

It is now time to look at the symptoms which develop when all these conditions are fulfilled.

1. There is *depression of mood*. This may vary from a certain greyness or dolefulness, a certain carewornness which the patient recognises to be unjustified; through a sense of unhappiness like a schoolboy's homesickness, with an embarrassing readiness to tears in both sexes; to frankly suicidal thoughts or actions. The lighter mood is accompanied by sighing respiration, a tendency to murmur 'oh dear, oh dear' for no very good reason, and a general lack of interest or pleasure in one's usual pursuits. As one goes down through the range of depressions, the patient becomes more and more withdrawn, sitting in silence and gazing at nothing, the state of mind excellently described by a mediaeval theologian: 'There is nothing new, and nothing true, and nothing matters.' In the severe depression the patient can hardly be roused to take an interest in anything around him or her.

One could include in this symptom a sense of vague anxiety, butterflies in the stomach, an irrational pessimism and an equally irrational emotional response. In depression the patient may feel that it is no use trying to visit anybody because the buses are always late, and anyway it's going to rain; or a normally rather reserved person may, to his own horror, be overwhelmed with tears by reading in the paper about some minor and distant tragedy. To him, a small earthquake in Chile is an overwhelming sadness.

This needs to be distinguished from a more natural unhappiness arising from genuinely depressing circumstances: from the daily news, for instance, often depressing enough; from the conditions of business; from the behaviour of teenage children; from an unhappy love affair, an uncongenial job or a disastrous marriage. This distinction can be difficult: but as a start this depression is usually commensurate with the cause; these patients do not say 'I have nothing to be depressed about' (see page 21); they recognise that their depression is largely rational. Moreover, the other symptoms described below are usually absent; when they are present one can say that unhappiness has turned into illness; and the more I see of true depression, the more precise I become in my criteria of diagnosis.

A special case of this justified depression is of course the grief of bereavement. No one can say what degree of depression is 'commensurate' with the loss of a beloved relation or friend, and in this extreme of grief the symptoms are often those of the fully developed true depression. I do not think the physiological approach to depression is applicable to acute grief, nor can it be treated as outlined below. Time is as so often the great healer; such physical aids as vitamins and perhaps sleeping pills for a while help; but eventually this has got to be got through with the loving help of the other survivors. Much has been written in the last few years on the subject of bereavement and grief, and most of it is very helpful.

It seems, judging from the pooled experience of very large numbers of people, that grief may last up to eighteen months or two years. If it continues beyond this sort of time then it may indeed have turned into a true depression and require treatment. But this diagnosis, like that of all depression and miseries, is not necessarily easy, and I hope this booklet will not be used as a manual of self-diagnosis: more as a manual of self-help.

2. There is *disturbed sleep pattern*. Typically the patient gets off to sleep well enough but wakes at two or three in the

morning in the depths of despair, and cannot sleep again. Less typically he or she has difficulty in getting off to sleep, lying awake perhaps for hours, possibly even all night; or sleeping and waking at intervals all through the night. Often the patient is in no very great distress during this time, probably tired and quite comfortable but with no sense whatever of approaching sleep. 'It is,' a patient said, 'as if I'd forgotten how to sleep.'

Least typically the patient may oversleep or hibernate. I have known patients sleep sixteen or eighteen hours a day, and this has always seemed to me a very understandable expression of depression, a way of escaping from the anxieties and responsibilities of life. In the case of one young woman, the first sign of improvement was that when her husband went to work, she no longer got back into bed.

3. There is *reversed diurnal variation*. This pompous phrase means simply that we are at what we laughingly call our best in the morning and decline slowly as the day goes on. In the typical depressive picture, this is sharply reversed; the patient wakes at whatever time, feeling like death physically as well as mentally; and by six or eight in the evening she is feeling a great deal better, able to enjoy a social evening, and reckons she needn't see the doctor in the morning. And then, of course, in the morning there it is waiting again.

This produces a bewilderingly mercurial effect in the inexperienced patient (and of course the first time we are all inexperienced) as the mood swings from misery to relative content; and it illustrates the way these symptoms (for they are *only* symptoms, as a cough is a symptom of bronchitis) can take over one's whole rational being. A patient went on holiday, well on in recovery from a depression, and woke the first few days at a normal sort of time, but full of foreboding that the holiday was a mistake. What folly to come *here* at *this* time or indeed at all, he thought. But by ten o'clock each morning these thoughts had quite disappeared and the rest of the day was of cloudless enjoyment. By the third day he had learnt to ignore his early morning gloom and wait for the later improvement.

4. There is *intellectual retardation*. This is the most bewildering and appalling of the symptoms, and leads many patients to the conviction that they are going mad. Memory, concentration and decision-making deteriorate to an extent quite unbelievable to anybody who has not experienced it. A man may ask an acquaintance his name three or four times in half an hour, and still not know who he was. A normally competent housewife will go out to buy three things and forget two of them. Patients forget the names of objects, where things are kept, where their children are at school.

Many patients report having to read the same column of print over and over again before they can understand and absorb it, and even then they forget what they have read within half an hour. After talking to a depressed patient it becomes clear that he or she has great difficulty taking in even quite a simple conversation, and has to bring attention back to the speaker over and over again by a conscious effort.

The failure of decision-making is even more frightening for the patient: a housewife may be reduced to tears by having to choose between this chop or that in a supermarket: an otherwise fit young soldier, taking a short and simple walk near his own home, came to a fork in the path on the way home, was quite unable to decide which fork to take, and ended up in tears beside the path, quite convinced he was going mad. A senior executive may spend all day at his desk shuffling papers from side to side but quite unable to take any action about any of them. One not infrequently hears of senior managers and directors who keep their juniors waiting for days for decisions and have clearly lost any ability to decide.

Sometimes the ability to take important or professional decisions is spared, and this is an example of arousal which I shall discuss further on; but even in these cases small decisions such as 'Do you want your egg poached or boiled?' may throw the patient into a positive panic. The failure of memory and concentration leaves the patient feeling that his or her brain has evaporated; and the failure of decision-making induces a panic-stricken helplessness which feels like insanity.

5. There is *physical retardation*. The patient is unduly tired in every sense of the phrase. He may be tired all day, waking tired, exhausted by mid-afternoon, never rising above a certain flat level of lassitude. One of the earliest signs of improvement is when the patient is able to say, 'Well, I'm getting through the day rather better.'

In addition, specific tasks become much harder work; a housewife may find carrying the vacuum cleaner upstairs almost more than she can do; and an otherwise perfectly fit young man is exhausted by a reasonably short walk. Here again the patient is alarmed and bewildered by the failing in her usual physical vigour, and fears she may be seriously ill. Indeed, this is one of the symptoms that most often bring depressed patients to the doctor.

The appetite may fall off enormously, so that even chewing becomes more trouble than it is worth; though in accordance with the principle that the hypothalamic functions may shift either 'up' or 'down', some patients eat more and put on weight in depression, a further cause for them to be depressed. One young patient who suffered recurrent depressions and learnt to know them very well used to come and see me, saying, 'I've started eating again: I must be depressed', usually rightly.

In severe cases the body temperature falls, the skin takes on a greasier texture, the patient becomes constipated, women's periods may cease and there may be an actual muscular inability to smile. In extreme cases the body becomes so retarded that the patient may remain in whatever bizarre position he has adopted until someone comes and moves him back.

A particularly distressing aspect of physical retardation is the fact that depressed women normally go off sex, to the extent that one can say that a woman who has suddenly gone off sex is depressed until proved otherwise. This of course is a great cause of unhappiness and misunderstanding in a marriage or love affair, and of further misery and self-blame for the patient. Her partner, unless he is unusually understanding or knowledgeable, is going to find it hard to accept that she has simply lost her taste for what was once a great pleasure, and is likely to believe that she has gone off not sex but *him*; while the patient, self-punishing as depressives always are, will be bitterly aware of failure, and find this further cause for self-blame. Moreover, in old-fashioned consideration of the illness, this is liable to get subtly confused with the post-Freudian emphasis on sex as the cause for everything, with further failure of understanding of the illness.

Similarly, men may become impotent, though in my experience this is rather less common than frigidity in women. Its secondary effects, however, are at least as upsetting, partly because many men's self-respect and indeed whole personality depend to some extent on their potency; sexual failure seems the ultimate humiliation in a man whose self-respect is already in rags; and partly because, while a loyal wife can and often does pretend an orgasm when she is not in fact aroused, a man can make no such pretence, and the same distresses and suspicions are aroused.

6. The sixth cardinal symptom is not necessarily the most bewildering to a patient but certainly the most distressing, and probably the one most likely to lead to suicide. This is a *sense of guilt*, or self-blame or feeling of unworthiness. This may be expressed in the milder cases as, 'But I've nothing to be depressed *about*; I'm not doing my job properly, I'm a burden to my family, I ought to pull myself together, what use

is a middle-aged woman?' In severer cases, and those where the trigger is some event such as a bereavement, guilt will focus on some more specific self-accusation, some failure to the deceased, some mistake the patient has made in his business, some shortcoming in a woman's handling of her family or home.

In more severe depression, the guilt becomes truly awful, invading the patient's every minute, waiting by her bedside, standing by his plate. It is always irrational and sometimes bizarre. A young woman explained to me coolly and calmly why it was her fault that her little boy had died: though there was no earthly reason to think so in fact. A young officer invalided out of the army in 1946 was obsessed by the conviction that he had to spend the rest of his life expiating his guilt for the war. Religious obsession, or the infinitely distressing loss of faith may spring from this sense of guilt, and the religious person may well express this to himself as a sense of eternal damnation.

This sense of guilt is also directed at the illness itself, and becomes shame at being ill. We have seen that the depressive is a conscientious and hard-working person, with high standards of conduct; and he or she has the utmost difficulty reconciling the apparent weakness or failure of the illness with his or her self-image as an effective and reliable person. This sense of shame prevents the patient talking about the illness to those around, confiding in her family or even going to see her doctor. An experienced depressive told me that when his illness is severe he does not let his wife, an equally experienced and sympathetic woman, see him taking his pills; but as the illness improves, he minds about this less and less until he is able to be quite open with her. It is not too much to say that this book is written primarily to help relieve this sense of guilt and shame.

6

Other symptoms of depression

Chapter 5 has outlined the six cardinal symptoms; diagnostic-ally I believe disturbed sleep pattern, intellectual retard-ation and self-blame to be the three most important, and I rarely diagnose depression in their absence. Curiously enough, overtly depressed mood may not be very marked; some psychiatrists talk about the 'smiling depression' in which other symptoms, including for instance bodily pains, may be much more important.

Not all symptoms are present in every case as with every other illness; and the severity of any one symptom compared with the others can be immensely variable. Experience and careful judgement are needed in those cases which do not show the full house of classical symptoms; and one should be slow to diagnose depression where the story is not a pretty clear one.

Some symptoms can go 'the other way' from expected: we have seen in the case of sleep pattern and in appetite that ac-tivity can be increased or decreased: though there is a classi-cal pattern, the patient *may* eat or sleep more or less. Similarly in some cases of 'depression', the patient is excited, ebullient and optimistic, in a great state of overactivity both mental and physical. This is the condition of mania or hypo-mania, and is at first sight difficult to reconcile with the gloomy and withdrawn picture of more typical depression. But mania and depression are not two different things: they are simply different points on a sliding scale of altered behav-iour, like the difference between hot and cold, or a sliding volume control on an amplifier. Sometimes the patient will swing between depression and ebullience, and this I shall discuss later as manic depression. But both are as it were different sides of the same coin.

There are of course other symptoms that occur in depressed patients, in many cases every bit as alarming to patient and family alike, but perhaps rather less uniformly presented, more often seen in other conditions such as anxiety state or schizophrenia and thus less absolutely typical of depression.

Panic attacks. These are sudden excesses of terror, brought on sometimes by some small event but often entirely spontaneous. Sometimes the effort of decision-making may bring on an attack; a teenager may rush from the room when presented with strangers; it may compound and increase the fears of a phobic state (see below). But equally it may come on quite without reason, a panic fear of nothing, from nowhere, when the patient is under no particular stress, perhaps sitting quietly or doing familiar things in familiar surroundings.

It is the 'tiger under the bed', the childish fear of the dark, totally irrational terror; and it may be so severe as to make the patient temporarily uncontrollable. Happily it does not usually last long; but while it does, to make things worse, the patient is not only filled with fear but is also terrified to feel himself so taken over.

The presence of friends and family undoubtedly helps here, and the patient is much more liable to panic attacks when she is by herself. This is perhaps the symptom with which those around can most help, not by telling the patient to pull herself together, which merely amounts to rejection of the symptom as real, but by accepting, by soothing and calming, and by generally making the patient feel safer.

Paranoia. People go off people, either the whole human race or an individual person. An experienced patient said to me, 'I go off somebody in each depression; luckily it's been a different person each time.' This may amount to a certain grumpiness or bad temper in dealing with their friends and family; it may include more serious delusions of relationship. The patient may believe his or her spouse is having an affair. Depressed patients will sometimes think that people are looking at them oddly or talking about them; there may be a curious degree of self-consciousness in public, particularly if the patient is wearing an unaccustomed garment or has some physical feature that is felt to be conspicuous. A request for plastic surgery to a nose or an ear *may* prove to be a symptom of depression.

Fairly rarely, depressed patients may present so elaborate a system of delusions and persecution as to raise grave difficulties in differentiating depression from schizophrenia; and this as we shall see can be all the more difficult where there are hallucinations.

Obsessional ruminations. This has two forms which should perhaps almost be treated separately. On the one hand, arising probably from the paranoia I have just mentioned, the patient may go endlessly over some slight or deprivation which rationally he knows perfectly well to be untrue. One woman said, 'I think everybody's getting sex except me; though I know it isn't true.' And a man found himself most uncharacteristically obsessed with money and how little he was paid: though he also knew perfectly well that he was a good deal better off than most people, and suffered additional guilt and self-blame for what he regarded as an absurd and self-indulgent delusion.

The other form seems to spring from a curious selectivity shown by the memory in depression, remembering all the bad things from the past and forgetting all the good; so that the depressed patient may be haunted by some peccadillo of the past which returns with such a sense of shame and pain that a driver may shut her eyes at seventy-five miles an hour. Examples are some awful thing you said to your aunt when you were six; or a cup you broke when you were twelve; or a minor unkindness done thoughtlessly years ago to someone who thought nothing of it at the time. They may stab the patient's conscience like a major sin.

Loss of self-confidence. This curiously selective memory undermines the patient's personality in many ways. We make sense of present experience and the anticipated future by comparing it with the remembered past. People whose memories are wholly unhappy tend to be unenterprising (or desperate) about future projects as they only have failure or unhappiness on which to build. Similarly depressed patients remember mainly their failures and unhappiness, and forget the successes and happiness which tend to be the bulk of our normal memories. (Usually we select mildly the other way.)

So they cannot bring themselves to face new people, try new enterprises, go to new places. Even seeing people they know or tackling familiar jobs may be beyond them, as all this is coloured by memories, however vague, of past failure. It is obviously made worse by the depressed mood and by the intellectual retardation I have already described; but this lack of self-confidence may be quite marked even in depression whose symptoms are quite mild.

Hypochondria. I am not sure this deserves status as a symptom on its own. It is an off-shoot partly of the pessimism described under depressed mood, partly of the insecurity and loss of confidence I have just described, and perhaps partly of the sense of guilt that is so marked and distressing a symptom. The patient feels because he is guilty, he deserves no trivial illness, and this must be something serious.

Some people are always hypochondriac: but in depression patients who have sailed resolutely in the past through illnesses, scares and dangers, become demoralised over some trivial symptom in themselves or their family. It is very striking how a previously robust-minded woman patient will suddenly start ringing her doctor every time the children cough, or over worries she would have taken in her stride a few months before; or a usually placid and stable man may become feverishly concerned about minor pain or because he has just discovered some bony promontory which has in fact always been there. The change is so great it is almost diagnostic for the alert doctor.

Physical symptoms. On the other hand, some depressed patients present with vague aches and pains (and other physical symptoms) which are not hypochondriac in the true sense of the word. Most typically these occur in the lower abdomen and legs; but they are not all that uncommon in other parts of the body, and may be related to previous injury.

It is sometimes found that following an injury the pain persists quite a long time after one would normally expect it to have cleared up. When physical complications have been excluded (and 'compensation neurosis' when this applies) there is a strong possibility that the injury has caused or triggered a depression of which the continuing pain is a symptom.

Pain and other physical reactions may also occur without injury; I have seen a woman patient with a mild paralysis of the legs of the type called hysterical, whose paralysis cleared up quickly on explanation and reassurance, to be followed only a few weeks later by an overt depression. Patients with long-standing headache or intractable backache may be found to be depressed, after years of treatment of all sorts including osteopathy and faith healing.

Properly enough, a doctor's first assumption is that pain has an organic origin; and certainly examination, and investigations and tests if necessary, must be made in pursuit of this diagnosis and to exclude organic causes. No pain is wholly imaginary. On the other hand, it is not good enough to say that as no organic cause has been found, the pain must be psychiatric in origin. This is diagnosis by exclusion, and almost always bad medicine. Depression as I am trying to show is a positive diagnosis based on definite symptoms, and in these cases of mysterious pain needs as firm a diagnosis as in any other case.

Phobic states. These are good examples of symptoms that may or may not be present in depression, and may well be found in other quite unrelated conditions. The two commonest in depression are agoraphobia and claustrophobia.

The former is a fear of open spaces, and is demonstrated by the patient's unwillingness to leave the house and venture into the open public space. Often there is a sort of radius in the patient's mind, five yards from the door, a hundred yards from the door, half a mile from the door, beyond which she will not venture; and the close relation between this fear and the main illness is shown by the fact that very often as the illness improves, the patient will venture farther and farther abroad. It has always seemed to me a very understandable symptom in depression, related to lack of confidence, withdrawal, inability to face people, the need of a secure base and a general tendency to crawl into a hole and pull it down after you. On occasion the agoraphobia may become tied to one precise locality or function: an intelligent young woman on two separate occasions came to me complaining of diarrhoea, which on further enquiry proved in fact to be a morbid fear of moving far from the lavatory, a kind of localised agoraphobia, and in common with her other symptoms depressive in origin.

Claustrophobia, the fear of being shut in, is perhaps more often found in depression than agoraphobia, but is also quite common in people who are not depressed. It may show itself in a small room, or in a lift, or in a small room only with the door shut. It may show itself in fairly large but indisputably closed spaces like aircraft or tube trains; and it may occur in crowded places like shops, churches or theatres, sometimes coming on only when the church or theatre doors are shut. Curiously enough, patients seem more worried by claustrophobia in the light than in the dark, presumably because they can actually see the feared enclosure.

Crippling as agoraphobia is, claustrophobia is almost worse, as it precludes the patient from many social activities and almost all travel. Some people cannot travel in cars in the back, or wearing a seat belt: and others have a variable claustrophobia which may clear completely for weeks, and then come on as suddenly as hiccups when they can least cope with it. It should be emphasised that if a patient's depression is better but he remains claustrophobic, this state may require quite different and separate treatment on its own; fear of specific objects like cats, spiders or pigeons is not characteristic of depression.

Depersonalisation. This is a weird and puzzling symptom which may occur in depression but is certainly not exclusive to it. It is not a serious symptom, being often experienced by perfectly fit people; but it is so odd, and such a tiresome addition to a depressed patient's other burdens that it requires a paragraph of explanation.

People find it very difficult to describe what it feels like, rather helplessly using loose terms like light-headed, fuzzy or even giddy. In fact the patient is not at all giddy or faint, he feels perfectly steady on his feet, and perception of sight and sound are in no way interfered with. But there is a subtle alteration of relationship with his surroundings; he is there and yet not there, as if watching unobserved, though he is able to continue meeting and talking to people who notice no change. The most readily accepted description is 'as if there were a block of plate glass between you and the rest of the world'. This best expresses the sense of 'one remove' the patient feels, the dream-like unreality in a perfectly normal world; and the mere recognition of this symptom by the doctor, with the automatic reassurance that it is not uniquely bizarre, is usually enough to set the patient's mind at rest.

Hallucinations. A hallucination is a gross visual error arising in the patient's brain; it is to be distinguished from an optical illusion, where the brain merely misinterprets real objects correctly seen, and from day-dreaming when visual memory may be so sharp as to create the impression of something really seen. A hallucination seems absolutely real to the patient: it may be bizarre or ordinary, reassuring, pleasant or frightening; but the patient has no doubt at that moment that it is real, though she will realise as soon as it disappears that it was unreal, and be frightened. Hallucinations are particularly associated with schizophrenia and certain drugs, cerebral tumours and the cerebral changes of old age; but they occur in depression and tend to be of a fairly characteristic sort.

People are startled, alarmed and puzzled to learn that hallucinations may occur in depression; their association, as we have seen, with major mental illness and cerebral change makes it at first sight very difficult to fit them into the general depressive symptoms. But in the symptom of guilt or self-blame, and in the curious adverse selection of memory that leads to the pessimism, hypochondria and lack of self-confidence of this illness, we see a gross error of self-perception. We still do not know enough brain physiology to tell which part of the brain is involved in these delusions of guilt and incompetence; but if this same error of self-perception is inserted into some part of the optic nerve system, then it will be expressed not in guilt or gloom, but in vision; and indeed in the typical depressive hallucination the patient sees a distorted vision of himself.

Quite a lot of people have had the experience of watching

themselves waking in bed, as it were from a corner of the ceiling; and patients may briefly see themselves, usually from above, walking along the street. One man said that at meals or waking in the morning he was vaguely aware that somebody else was there; and as the illness got better this sense of presence became more shadowy and infrequent.

In one particular patient hallucinations were the symptoms that brought him to see me; they were frequent, varied and convincing, some with the element of self-perception I have described but some either irrelevant to self-perception or schizoid and frightening. In one instance of the former, he was sitting writing, and found himself holding not a pen but a wrist and hand that were themselves holding a pen. In another instance he became aware in the room of a large aluminium tube about eight feet long and two feet in diameter, which he realised quite clearly was himself. In each case the vision was solid and unalarming, until it cleared, when he realised what had happened and was very frightened.

Hallucinations, like many of the other symptoms in this section, are not typical of or exclusive to depression; and will always raise in the doctor's mind a wide selection of possible diagnoses, of which depression is only one.

7

Variations of depression

The type of depression which we are discussing is usually called reactive depression; and curiously this has not passed into popular medical legend. Endogenous depressions and manic-depressive swings have somehow caught the popular imagination with much greater liveliness. They are certainly more dramatic, and perhaps better meet the modern taste for the romantic and the mysterious.

Endogenous depression should mean depression occurring without any predisposing cause beyond the patient's own personality. It undoubtedly occurs; the tendency of depressions, like peptic ulcers, to be worse in the spring and autumn suggests an endogenous rather than external cause. But it is very rare indeed to find a totally spontaneous depression without any stress or trigger that one can see. Again, one will never find a depression except in a personality inclined towards it, as can sometimes be seen years in advance, and this inclines towards the endogenous; but the reactive element is almost always to be found. In any case the features of depression are so similar in the endogenous or the reactive form that I do not find it a particularly useful distinction.

Similarly manic-depressives are happily pretty rare in general practice. In all specialties of medicine hospital doctors see the rarities and the severe cases because these are the ones that are filtered off to them by GPs; so hospital practice has a quite unworldly bias towards the rare and severe.

The manic-depressive illness takes two forms: it may occur

in circumstances when one would expect a straight reactive depression, and is the equivalent of other functional shifts that move 'up' rather than moving 'down'. We have already seen this in the case of sleep pattern, where the expected insomnia is sometimes replaced by oversleeping, and of appetite which may go either way in depression.

Here the patient goes into an up-swing (mania or hypomania, minor mania) where others would go into a down-swing, and in very similar circumstances; and in this case hypomania should be regarded as the other side of the coin from depression. To understand this requires the same sort of mental adjustment as realising that hallucinations are merely delusions made visible. We have seen more than once that the functional shift within the hypothalamus, though usually in the direction of depression or inhibition, may be in the direction of excitation, and mood is no exception to this.

Other patients show a more truly endogenous, steady wave-like swing up and down over weeks or months, sometimes with remarkable regularity. This is the manic-depression of popular understanding. The swings may be slight, between an unusual feeling of fitness and well-being and a certain dullness and tiredness; or they may be violent, between a deep weeping depression and a state of uncontrollable excitement and overactivity. In certain rare cases the cycle may be frighteningly short, the patient swinging from one extreme to the other several times in the course of a single day.

The swings themselves, the height/depth of the troughs and crests, also vary greatly. A patient may swing up from 'normal' into elation and down again; or from 'normal' into depression and up again; or either side of 'normal' into elation and depression, and these again may vary greatly in severity.

The up or manic swing differs markedly from the down or depressive in that the patient tends to lose insight. Most depressed patients know there is something wrong with them, even if at first they think it is a moral failure rather than an illness; but the hypomanic patient is having a wonderful time, dashing about, spending money, laughing hugely, understanding all the problems of the universe, foreseeing a marvellous future, often hugely sexy and not infrequently very good company to his or her friends, if a trifle exhausting. Sometimes the state is frightening; an experienced patient will realise she is high, and come to the doctor; but much of the time it is hardly surprising the patient sees no need for a doctor and indeed resents the poor fellow's well-meaning attempts to interfere. 'You're jealous of me,' said a patient, 'because I'm so happy'; and indeed there was a measure of truth in what he said.

Lay people often confuse manic-depression with schizophrenia, and considering the extraordinary twin personality manic-depressives may present this is not surprising, given an equal misunderstanding of both illnesses. But, briefly, schizophrenia describes as it were a horizontal split between the conscious and sub-conscious mind, so that the patient misinterprets the errant thoughts and impressions that bubble into our minds, as we say 'from nowhere'; whereas the 'vertical' split between Dr Jekyll and Mr Hyde shows the manic and the depressed or probably normal phases of a manic-depressed personality. Stevenson made a good fanciful story out of traits he probably observed in his own personality.

Happily there are these days very effective drugs with minimal side-effects that both control hypomania, and dampen the swings to and fro, so that a manic-depressive patient or one with hypomanic swings can lead a much more normal and predictable life, without his family and employers living in constant fear of a sudden burst of ill-judged overactivity, extravagance and irresponsibility.

8

Premenstrual and menopausal depression; anorexia

Premenstrual depression is an important subject for three reasons: it is usually easily treated, it may monthly bedevil the life of a whole family, and until fairly recently a large number of women thought they were the only people in the world to suffer from it. If the recent discovery of 'the premenstrual syndrome' by the drug firms has done nothing else it has shown many women they are not alone in their trouble and it can be treated.

Although the symptoms are very similar to those of the true reactive depression, it is in fact different in kind. Its regular and predictable appearance before the period demonstrates its hormonal basis; irritability and tension as is well known may be its most marked feature; and in many women there is a remarkable lack of insight. In many cases it is the husband who approaches the doctor, often with some such remark as 'She just can't see that she makes our lives a misery one week a month.'

The classical view of premenstrual tension and depression, for over forty years to my certain knowledge, is that it is due to retention of fluid before the period. Fluid is retained in the abdomen which accounts for the bloating that many women are aware of, and in the breasts which partly accounts for their greater size. This comes as no surprise to many girls who are aware of passing less urine than usual before the period, and then making up for it once the period starts. Some women have to keep underwear in two sizes, premenstrual and postmenstrual.

Fluid is also retained in the cerebral cortex, and it is the water-logging here that leads to the premenstrual symptoms that can be so extraordinarily marked in some women. Exactly why this causes tension or depression is not quite clear, but it does give a very clear rationale for the classical treatment.

This is by a diuretic, a pill that makes one pass more water, and women with regular predictable periods are able to take this for a week or ten days before the period. This as I have suggested is a pretty old-fashioned treatment but answers very well in a large number of cases where the period is predictable. The dose varies: some girls take one every morning for a week; some take one every three days for ten days before the period. Each woman has to establish her own régime, and many find it completely satisfactory. It is less helpful where the periods are irregular; but here sometimes the girl can spot the onset of premenstrual symptoms, and start the pills in time.

Recently, as I have said, the drug firms have suddenly discovered premenstrual depression and have launched great campaigns advocating a number of profitable treatments with hormones. These are certainly available where other methods fail, and certainly some girls on the Pill find it improves their premenstrual symptoms. But it is a pretty sound principle not to use hormones unless one has to, and there are, happily, simpler methods.

Another more recent treatment is the use of vitamin B6 (pyridoxine). This has been found remarkably helpful in this condition, and has the great advantage that no accusations of side-effects have as yet been made. It is supposed to be taken according to a fairly elaborate timetable from the fifth to the twenty-sixth day of the cycle; but there is really no great point in this, and it can be taken steadily all the way through in a dose of 200 milligrams (mg) a day, a great boon to women whose periods are not regular.

The menopause is greatly connected with depression in popular legend; indeed, 'It's that time of life for her' is given half contemptuously as a reason for almost any behaviour in any woman between forty and sixty. I cannot say that I have found depression to be a frequent accompaniment of the change of life, nor the menopause a frequent feature of depression in women. Most of the depressed women I have seen have been well before the menopause; and those women of menopausal age whom I have seen in depression have presented all those familiar features of reactive depression, and responded to the customary treatment.

That sex hormones can influence depression there is no doubt. Girls on the Pill may get depressed, often with a regular mid-cycle pattern, and if a depressed girl is on the Pill it is often sound medical practice to take her off it while treatment is being given. I have known depressed women respond definitely if temporarily to treatment with hormones; but in each case that I have in mind full recovery only followed the use of the true antidepressants.

Depression after childbirth, as we have seen, is probably partly traumatic like the mild and transient depression that follows most operations. But its regularity and relative severity seem to suggest that the hormonal element is a strong one, though when it persists into a long-lasting post-partum depression (and I have met one woman whose child was then aged 23) the antidepressants are the proper and most effective treatment.

Perhaps the saddest form of depression is that seen in old people, in whom it earns such unpleasant names as senile depression or involutional melancholia. It differs from depression in the younger patient in two particular features: to be old is to be deprived, of friends, faculties and future; and while a hale and happy old age is perfectly possible, there are permanent obstacles to the older patient's recovery, and a permanent inclination in the older (and particularly the widowed) towards depression.

Secondly, the ageing brain is already less efficient; arteriosclerosis, the narrowing and hardening of the arteries which in fact starts in one's teens, slows the brain and imposes on it deterioration of function some of which is not unlike depression.

Nevertheless, it would be both callous and medically incorrect to dismiss gloomy old people as just gloomy old people. Such patients may respond to the right antidepressant, and indeed often respond almost equally well to the withdrawal of the wrong drug previously prescribed. Many an elderly person has slipped imperceptibly into withdrawal and inactivity, and has been rescued from this state once it has been recognised. Sometimes merely stimulation, the company of other people, new interests and activity are enough; but the right prescription can make an astonishing difference to the patient, who may seem to shed years in a matter of weeks.

The last variant of depression to be mentioned is anorexia nervosa. There is a lot of discussion among doctors about the cause and nature of this illness, whether it is in fact a form of depression, or a form of schizophrenia, or quite unrelated to either of these conditions: and severe anorexia is outside the scope of this book. Nevertheless, a mild anorexia has so many depressive features, and responds so well to conventional antidepressant treatment that it merits a brief discussion.

It is a condition typically found in young women in their twenties; it may start as early as puberty, and I have come across one case where, in a modified form, it lasted all the woman's life into old age. It occurs occasionally in men.

The girl becomes convinced she is fat, and ceases to eat; and she will go to bizarre lengths to avoid eating, and to deceive those who are trying to get her to eat. She may eat, and then go and make herself vomit; she may take huge doses of laxative to make the bowels overact and thus lose both fluid and nourishment. She conceals her not eating the way an alcoholic conceals drink.

In the fully developed illness the patient becomes horrifyingly thin, a scarecrow figure from the concentration camps. She remains immensely active, and it is a curious feature of the illness that the patient very rarely catches a cold. Her periods cease, and occasionally are never re-established. If the illness goes on long enough the patient may die of starvation, or her metabolism may be so damaged as never to return to normal.

All through this the girl believes she is fat; there is a distortion of body-image, and this may remind us of the other distortions of self-perception in depression, the delusion of guilt and the hallucinations. Most people can indicate with their hands, and with their eyes shut, the width of their heads, their shoulders and their waists pretty correctly; an anorectic girl will get the first two right but may wildly over-estimate the silhouette of her waist, by six or nine inches. Interestingly, in treatment of the mild cases, this estimate becomes more correct as the girl gets better.

Most patients with anorexia need specialist treatment, probably in hospital. But it is possible to find cases that are early enough or mild enough to treat as depression, and these may be saved from progressing to the most serious form of the illness. Any girl with a tendency to depression who starts worrying obsessionally or disproportionately about her weight, and who goes off her food to any marked degree is at risk of anorexia; and sympathetic attempts should be made to get her to see a doctor. This may be difficult as the illness only seems to occur in the most obstinate of patients, and of course as her parents become more and more frantic with worry, the patient becomes more determined to lose weight.

I heard of one patient cured by a beach photographer in the seaside town where she lived. He insisted on photographing her as she hurried down to the beach in her bikini, and later thrust the developed print into her unwilling hand. She was so shocked by what she saw in the unfamiliar context of a street photograph that her body-image was restored, and she at last saw herself as thin. The patient developed a severe depression later in life.

9

Treatment

I have a two-fold object in thus cold-bloodedly displaying these various symptoms. I want to bring home the message of Chapter 2; to convince the patient on the one hand that this is an illness no less than say duodenal ulcer, to be recognised by its own group of symptoms irrespective of cause or theory, as readily as any other organic disease; and on the other hand by laying out the patient's symptoms to show him or her that this is indeed the diagnosis, this is not an arcane and profound moral failure but a true illness, and that the world is full of fellow-sufferers.

It can also be immensely helpful to explain to the family or household the mechanism of the illness. They see a friend or relation gradually or suddenly slipping into an apparently quite alien pattern of behaviour. The tower of strength weeps; the brisk executive cannot make up his mind; the splendid wife and mother becomes withdrawn, unresponsive, lazy, lackadaisical, even dirty. It is an enormous relief to those around to learn something of the illness; dealing with depression in one's own family is extremely difficult (far more difficult than being the doctor) and we shall have more to say about this later on: but a simple description of the illness is a vital first step.

When one comes to discuss the actual treatment of depression one has all too often to re-open the nineteenth-century moral arguments to which I referred at the beginning of this book. People who seem to have broadly accepted the organic view of depression in its description and diagnosis, raise again moral qualms about its being treated organically.

This is partly because the depressive is a self-reliant and (especially when ill) self-punishing personality; she feels she does not deserve treatment; and wishes to be left to continue the fight alone. It is partly a mistaken and by now rather old-fashioned belief that 'mental' illness must have 'mental' treatment.

There is also a confused muddled Northern puritanism, feeling that pills are wrong, it can't be that easy, it's all in the mind, isn't it; and this latches on to an even more complicated muddle, this strange modern nihilism and mysticism in which people believe what is good cannot be either rational or simple. They feel that the occult and arcane is somehow more *real* than the physiological and straightforward; and that 'natural' methods are morally superior to medicines.

I can only refer you back to the beginning of the book. This is an organic illness, and the treatment of an acute depression is organic.

Psychotherapy of a very minor sort undoubtedly helps. The mere description and explanation of the illness relieves the patient's fear that he or she is going mad, and does something to raise the awful burden of guilt and restore the revaged self-respect that is a symptom of the illness. To live a life happy with oneself and with those around one it is necessary to love oneself just enough; the depressive is rarely at risk of loving himself too much, and a mild psychotherapy can often help the patient towards at least a wry acceptance of his own personality, tinged perhaps with a certain gallows humour.

Where there is severe disturbance of personality, lasting many years with disabilities by now deeply imbedded, deep psychotherapy or psychoanalysis may well have a place. But depressives, being basically of a very good personality, are rarely in need of having that personality altered: any more than a man with a broken leg needs his whole stature changed. The vast majority of depressions occur in patients of previously good personality (a psychiatric jargon phrase); and when the illness is better this personality reasserts itself.

Most illnesses get better of their own accord: eventually. In the generality of medicine, leaving out the dramas of surgery or the neat satisfactions of endocrinology, doctors cannot often hope to cure people who were not going to get better anyway.

But they can hope to get patients better quicker. Where the depression is mainly dependent on immediate and avoidable stress, recovery will start when the patient is removed from the stress. The *first* first-aid of a burn is to take your hand out of the fire. But often the patient cannot be removed from the stress of unending and unavoidable overwork or an ineluctable relationship; and often the illness has already gone too deep for a rapid relief; and in such cases an untreated depression may last literally for years.

Some of the post-war depressions lasted on and off for five or ten years. One or two patients treated for an acute depression apparently of a few months' standing have said on full recovery, 'I haven't felt like this for eleven or twelve years', and I remember a woman who had been in a varying post-partum depression since her last child was born twenty-three years before.

So treatment at least shortens the period of suffering; and at best can transform a life.

In a mild depression, the minor tranquillisers in remarkably small dosage for about a fortnight may keep the symptoms at bay while the patient does her own recovering. In a more severe depression the true antidepressants come into their own and these are in my view the proper treatment. They fall into two main groups, the mono-amine oxidase inhibitors, known by the rather Shakespearean initials MAOI, and the tricyclics and quadricyclics which can be grouped together as the imipramine derivatives.

Their action is closely similar; we have seen that in depression the hypothalamus at the base of the brain becomes deficient in a group of hormones known briefly as mono-amines; and there is good experimental evidence to suggest that these hormones are normally stored in the base of the brain, and in periods of excess activity are released and after serving their purpose destroyed by an enzyme called mono-amine oxidase. The MAOI drugs as their name suggests *inhibit* this mono-amine oxidase, the hormone is destroyed at a lower rate and its storage level is rebuilt in the brain cells.

In simple terms the sequence is as follows: the mono-amine hormones such as serotonin and noradrenaline which have so much to do with mood regulation are released from the stor-age cells during periods of activity. All hormones are rapidly destroyed in the blood by enzymes (or they would totally flood the system) and these are no exception; so that where there is a great out-pouring of the hormones there is also great destruction. When the levels of these hormones fall, there is a great deterioration in the efficiency of the hypotha-lamus, and what is called a functional shift of those activities which it regulates. The antidepressants come into the chem-ical reaction at this stage, and slow down the destructive ac-tivity of the enzymes, so that the mono-amine hormones are gradually restored by the normal metabolism of the brain.

Two things follow from this: firstly, cure is not overnight. The immediate effect of the antidepressants is nil. They are not psychotropic drugs, they have no short-term effect on the mood, like phenobarbitone or alcohol; they are neither pep pills nor sedatives, except in some cases as a side-effect. Their action is rather like that of iron in anaemia: if a patient is given iron he feels no benefit at first. But as the body takes the iron and utilises it in haemoglobin to carry the oxygen, the patient feels better. So I always warn patients that they may feel no change for two or three weeks. Some drugs work faster than others, and some patients respond quicker than others: but in general it is important for the patient to understand the likely course of events, and the doctor would be doing him no service if this were not made clear.

To some patients this is a blow; but surprisingly often the assurance that this is an illness and not a moral failure as he or she thinks, explanation along the lines that I have suggested and the assurance that treatment can be given do the patient so much good that he experiences quite a lift, sometimes for five or six days; and in any case is able to face the future with greater objectivity and patience.

Secondly, treatment has to be prolonged. Again rather like giving iron for anaemia, if treatment is stopped as soon as the patient feels better, then the biochemistry will again slide down the slope towards deficiency and illness. It is no good giving up just as the working level of iron or mono-amine has been achieved; treatment must be continued while, as it were, a reserve level builds up; and this may mean anything from six months to two years.

This again seems a disappointing prospect; but one is able to assure the patient that most of this time she will be on a maintenance dose of the drug, totally confident that she is going to get better and feeling so much better that the treatment is no anxiety.

A further interesting substance that can be used in the treatment of depression is L-tryptophan. This is the chemical precursor or raw material of 5-HT or serotonin (see Chapter 13) which is one of these important mono-amines mentioned in Chapter 4. L-tryptophan supplies the brain with raw material of 5-HT, enabling it to rebuild its own working level.

It can be used by itself or together with the medicines we have been mentioning, particularly in short-term treatment or in mild cases. It is usually prescribed for short periods of about three months; it has some side-effects like the other medicines but on the whole fewer and less uncomfortable. It does not seem to be very effective in all severe cases, or for long-term treatment.

Patients are always worried lest the treatment should prove addictive or habituating, and here it is very easy to reassure them. Addictive drugs have two characteristics in common: the user gets some immediate pleasure or benefit from their use, and their withdrawal causes an unpleasant reaction, needing a further dose of the drug to restore the user to a temporary fragile normality. A good example of this is the traditional 'hair of the dog that bit you', the stiff drink as the treatment of a hangover.

As already suggested the patient gets no immediate pleasure or benefit from the drug: for as much as ten days maybe it is as if the drug had no action at all and that is no way to cause addiction. There are no withdrawal effects in the ordinary sense, though suddenly and unwisely stopping the drug may bring a sharp return of the depression.

Moreover these drugs are even rather unpleasant to take. The MAOI drugs require careful restriction of diet: foods containing tyramine, an amine acid, have to be avoided, such as cheese, broad beans, meat and yeast extracts like Marmite and Bovril and most forms of alcohol among others.

All are liable to cause a dry mouth, and this is almost invariable; constipation which is frequent, and excessive sweating which is rather more rare. A very few people are made so drowsy that treatment has to be greatly slowed down at the beginning of the course; and if one goes up through the dose schedule too fast (for I believe in starting at a very small dose and working up over about ten days) then there is an extraordinary sense of aching tiredness in all the limbs, which can in fact be confused with the tiredness of depression. Sometimes the heart bumps about. So there is no incentive for the patient to continue treatment for a moment longer than the doctor suggests.

Above all the depressive is not of an addictive personality. She tends to be tough-minded and self-punishing, resisting the whole idea of treatment at all, inclined to accept the sufferings of depression as a due punishment for the guilt that is part of the illness. As soon as the patient begins to feel better she starts putting pressure on the doctor to reduce or withdraw the treatment, usually far too soon; and I cannot think of a single instance where I have had to insist on the patient's cutting her pills.

It is a very important part of the doctor's job in depression to satisfy the patient with his explanation, and to win his confidence with the steadiness and conviction with which these explanations are offered; and the family and household can greatly help the patient if they understand this description, and help the patient to accept it and base their support upon it.

Recovery is rarely absolutely straightforward. It is a matter of ups and downs, and even when the patient is warned of this, the down days or even hours are infinitely distressing. They engulf the patient's whole personality and there is little or no room for insight or optimism. As the weeks of recovery go by, however, and the patient is able, usually with help, to look back at her state when treatment was first started it is then possible to see that the general course of this zig-zag graph is upward. It is helpful and indeed important that notes should be kept of the precise symptoms when the patient first visited the doctor, and comparison of each particular symptom can then be made from week to week and month to month as treatment goes on; the patient is often surprised to be reminded how much progress she has made.

This is all the more important because the depressed patient is emotionally immensely vulnerable, and this instability continues during treatment and well into recovery. Little set-backs that would normally be taken in one's stride or hardly even noticed upset the patient totally. Often he recognises this as silly and irrational but can do little about it. A brief verbal brush with a fellow-driver that would normally merely irritate will plunge him into depression and self-blame for hours; and the fear that haunts the recovering patient is that the illness is going to start all over again.

However, with these warnings delivered, one can say that in general the physical symptoms get better first: the patient is less tired, appetite may improve, there may be an improvement in sleep with or without the help of other pills. Shaky agitation, butterflies in the stomach, symptoms such as these come in the same category but are slightly later in getting better; while the 'deep' physical symptoms such as the quite severe pains that may occur, may recover early *or* late in the treatment.

Secondly, the mood improves and the depression becomes easier. A man is no longer the victim of tears; a young woman said she no longer cried when people were nice to her; the urgency of suicidal thoughts gives way to a pretty grey acceptance of a life as a necessary burden or a duty. People even realise dimly that there are some pleasant aspects in life, even if they still feel themselves excluded; if there is not yet hope, there is at least endurance.

Many people are aware of an actual slow lift of spirits at this stage 'like a bubble climbing through the mud of a murky pond.' This stage of recovery may be as insidious as the onset of the disease, which can creep on the patient unawares over many weeks; so that after a month or so of treatment the patient, as we have seen, is surprised to realise how much better he is.

The mental or intellectual symptoms seem very often to recover last of all, and this is a distressing thought for a professional person trying to do a job or a housewife trying to run a house. Decision-making depends largely on self-confidence, and concentration will improve as the patient's withdrawal and self-absorption improve; but memory, while depending to some extent on concentration, seems most directly affected by physiological changes, and may well be the last of all to return to normal. By this time, however, the depressed mood is so much better, the patient is feeling so well and so confident of final recovery that these disabilities can be borne with comparative ease. Sometimes it may even become a rather bad-taste joke: 'Mum's memory again' sort of thing.

Sometimes one isolated symptom may linger for months after all else has recovered. The phobic states tend to fade slowly, probably because they are not entirely depressive in origin. A middle-aged woman recovered everything except her memory, which finally returned about six months after all other symptoms were better; and a younger woman by now well in all other ways was unable to recover her normal sexuality for some months. Then she suddenly and radiantly announced, 'I've fallen in love all over again': happily with the same man.

There are certain puzzling features of recovery which again it is valuable for the patient to know about. At a certain stage, about a third of the way through recovery, many patients go through a phase of increased dream activity. One cannot particularise more than that. Patients have said, 'my dreams are more interesting', or 'my dreams are more vivid', or on one occasion 'I now realise I dream in technicolour.' In a few cases these dreams are violent or nightmarish, and one patient reported dreams so terrifying that for ten days she was afraid to go to sleep. All this seems to represent a return to normal activity in the brain chemistry, and those acquainted with sleep research and dream research will recognise a similar pattern of increased dreaming after dream deprivation.

I do not myself subscribe to the belief of certain schools of psychotherapy that the *content* of dream is always and automatically significant in itself. Faith will always find out the bases of its own belief; to those without this faith the content of dreams seems irretrievably random. It is perfectly true that where one is profoundly preoccupied with some subject or problem distorted references to this may occur in one's dreams; and in the overstressed patient there may occur a curious divorce between the content and the emotion of dreams. A young soldier in a post-war depression had dreams about the war which were objectively horrifying: but in his dream observed, for instance, an enemy soldier walking down the road towards him with his face totally shot away, without any emotion at all. And on the other hand a patient may wake sweating, screaming or laughing from a dream that objectively described seems even to the dreamer not the least bit frightening or funny.

Secondly, when patients are well on in treatment and feeling a great deal better, they may report a curious flattening or neutralisation of emotion. They may for instance be aware of pleasurable circumstances without actually experiencing the pleasure one would expect; it seems second-hand, impersonal, remote. This is alarming to a patient who has already experienced the lack of response in profound depression, or the depersonalisation. I regard this as a sign that the patient is now on an adequate maintenance dose of the antidepressant, and can look forward both to continuing improvement in the depression, and to a steady lightening of this unnerving symptom as the treatment is tapered off.

Thirdly, the final stages of a depression, sometimes many weeks after recovery seems to be complete, may be marked by periods of intense irritability or tension lasting about twenty-four hours, issuing in bad-tempered and impatient behaviour to those around. These spells of bad temper may have a curious feature in common with the waves of passing depression in the up and down phase earlier in the illness, and that is that they may end quite suddenly and spontaneously. A patient described walking across a room in a down phase, and finding himself depressed on his left foot and not on his right; and in another patient where spells of great tension were indeed the only symptom at all, the abrupt way they lifted suggested the possibility that they might be due to depression.

10

Management (for the family only)

Treatment is the doctor's business, living with the patient is the family's, and I have *no* doubt the latter has the harder part. It is extremely difficult to handle depression in one's own household, even when one has acquired enough knowledge of the illness not to go through the cruel and useless business of telling the patient to pull himself together.

It requires great patience as a start. A patient in a depression, however much one loves him or her, is dull, repetitive and unreasonable. The withdrawn patient is quite unhandleable, sitting silent and still, a death's head at any feast. The constant lamentation over his fancied and morbid guilt with the best will in the world becomes monotonous; and it is quite impossible to frame a reply to the patient's miseries which is neither patronising nor exacerbating. One cannot agree that she is a drain on her friends and useless at her job: but it is hard to find any rational argument the other way.

In many years of trying to advise friends, families and lovers of depressed patients how best to support them I have found no really satisfactory formula. In general, remember you are dealing with an ill person who is going to recover; the sighs, tears and complaints are symptoms like a cough in pneumonia, and are temporary. The patient needs above all loving acceptance which will at the same time not make him feel a greater burden than he already feels, and an understanding which is not too cloying. Depressives are tough-minded people, and respond to the hardboiled physiological approach, so avoid sentimentality in your approach. Some people always hate being touched: but if the patient is not one of these, nothing is so reassuring as physical contact, except where the really depressed feel themselves literally unfit to be touched.

Expect sudden changes of mood: the recovering patient who agrees to an expedition or to have a visitor may find at the last moment she cannot face it, and a very careful balance has to be found between the gentle pressure that enables her to take another step into recovery, and the officious forcing into further stress that may set her back days. Remember the emotional vulnerability of the depressed.

The question whether a patient should remain at work or not is always a difficult one. Where he or she is much incapacitated there is no problem except to guard the patient against a further access of guilt. But a patient's work may be a stress *or* a support, a burden *or* a source of pride, a bore *or* the only source of interest or companionship she ever sees. The probable attitude of boss, juniors or workmates has to be considered; who will look after her at home; is home a pleasant place to stay? The real question is whether the patient will benefit more from the rest and relief from stress in staying away from work, than she will lose from the additional sense of failure and guilt this may engender, from loneliness and from boredom. Patients usually want to stay at work, and they are not usually the best people to make the decision. Few really busy offices can cope with a depressed person at work, and though the more enlightened ones try very well, it is like carrying a passenger on a warship, and comes hard on the rest of the crew.

In the same way the patient should not go on a convalescent holiday too soon; at the right moment it consolidates the recovery, at the wrong it wrecks the whole thing. There is no more bitter experience than to go off on an expensive and glamorous holiday (or indeed a cheap and cheerful one) and not to enjoy it.

In short, patients need first and foremost an intelligent understanding of their illness, in which their families can help to carry them confidently and patiently towards recovery. They need continuing loving acceptance as people, and an equally loving expectancy of their recovery. Argument and verbal reassurance are little or no use. Physical contact can be greatly reassuring and comforting, but love-making is likely to be a demand they cannot meet.

Patients and families always ask whether this illness is likely to recur. We have seen that like most other illnesses this is the product of a certain attack and a certain defence, the interaction between certain stresses and certain personalities. If a given block of concrete, dropped a given distance on to a given leg, will break it, then the same block dropped the same distance will break the same leg; and exactly the same stresses applied to the same personality will produce the same illness.

But this is unlikely. Many depressions are due to quite unusual stresses which the patient is unlikely to meet again; there may have been additional unrecognised factors such as an attack of flu or a girl being on the Pill. Above all the patient has changed: even if the threshold is once more surpassed, with increasing experience one learns to handle stress better. In particular the experience of the first or second depression is invaluable: a patient who first comes to the doctor bewildered, guilty, not knowing quite what to say, not knowing what complaint to make, full of self-blame for incompetence at his job and for being a burden at home, may come back some years later saying baldly, 'It's my depression again' as another patient may say 'It's my asthma'. I believe this to be the major benefit of the approach to depression I have outlined in this book.

11

Specialist treatments

In previous chapters I described what is to my mind the standard management of the average depression seen in general practice. Few of these cases need the help of a psychiatrist. But in any category of illness there are mild cases and severe, responsive and intractable ones, and this is equally true of depression. These severe, intractable or very long-lasting cases may need further treatment, and for completeness' sake I shall describe some of the methods used in these cases. It *must* be emphasised that these cases are the minority and these treatments are uncommon in the experience of any general practitioner.

Prolonged sedation may be used to tide the patient over a crisis in his illness. When a patient is already depressed, perhaps already under treatment, and the stress giving rise to the illness continues unabated, a halt can be called to the whole psychological and physiological process by putting him to sleep, or at least into a deep drowsiness, for several days. This was also an important first-aid in wartime breakdowns, when the rapid application of 'front line sedation' saved many psychological casualties from more serious illness later.

It is *not* a treatment of depression, it is a treatment of crisis, a sort of temporary dressing put on the wounded mind to protect it from the influences that are continuing to wound.

A specific treatment of depression is electroconvulsive therapy, ECT or shock treatment, which has had a very strange passage in popular medical mythology. It was first reported in the 1930s, and it was extensively used in the later

1940s and early '50s. At first it was a pretty crude affair: it is essential to the treatment that the patient should have an actual epileptic fit, and this was first done without anaesthetic or muscle relaxants. Later the procedure was carried out only under full anaesthetic and with muscle relaxants of the sort used in general surgery to prevent the injuries that may occur during an uncontrolled fit.

Some years later popular myth decided that ECT was a barbarous and unnecessary treatment, done by sadistic doctors who did not know what they were doing: and always making the patient worse. Had this view been put forward in the 1940s, there might have been something in it, except for the last bit, as even then profoundly depressed patients benefited hugely from the treatment. But it is very odd that this myth should have grown up at a time when the techniques of ECT have been refined and humanised beyond the dreams of early practitioners.

It is not a pleasant treatment: but then neither is having your gallbladder out. Few patients would wish to go through either procedure twice: though it was impressive before the days of drugs like lithium how many patients were willing to have monthly ECT rather than suffer recurrent depression. But in each case the long-term results may be spectacular, and the patient often ends up wishing he or she had had the treatment some years sooner.

The effect of the treatment seems to be to induce an emotional as well as an electrical storm in the patient's brain, after which the brain seems to be more free to resume normal patterns of thought.

The treatment is given very variably, sometimes six times in three or four weeks, sometimes at the same rate over a longer period, and occasionally daily for a short time. It is given when medicines have failed or partly failed, when the illness has been going on a long time and is deeply imbedded, when the illness is very severe, and when there is a crisis in the illness such as a sudden deterioration and severe risk of suicide. It is not a treatment of first resort: but many patients who have been ill for a long time may be restored to something approaching normal on ECT.

As an example, there was a young nurse who suffered recurrent severe depressions, brought on partly by her constant state of rebellion against authority. Every day for her was a fight. The depressions occurred not less than twice a year over many years, and though the drug treatments already mentioned eased the depressions and eventually cleared them, the situation was intolerable for the patient and everybody else. It was she who said while emerging from one depression 'I can't possibly go through all this again' and through all these years the risk of suicide was so close that the doctor actually come to doubt his moral right to prevent her.

She was determined even as depressives go; and it took five years to persuade her to see a psychiatrist and to go into hospital. Here she was offered ECT, and her GP more or less bullied her into accepting. Six months later she was off all treatment, and has for many years led a normally turbulent life coping splendidly and free of the incapacitating depressions she used to have.

It is thought that the convulsions and collapse of ECT are akin to the psychologically-induced commotion and collapse of abreaction, which though of little use in depression is still worth a mention here as an example of physiological method in the treatment of 'mental illness'.

The word abreaction dates from Freud's early studies, and refers to the blowing off of repressed emotion, under the influence of hypnotism or drugs or the powerful suggestion of psycho-analysis. It was used during and after the First World War in the treatment of such conditions as shellshock; and very extensively in the Second World War in the treatment of battlefield neurosis both from the battlefields themselves, and from the bombed cities. It was in this latter period that the connection was made between the phenomenon of abreaction and the work by Pavlov on the reaction of the brain in various degrees of stress. Pavlov's work on dogs, to which we shall refer in the chapter 'The Scientific Background', threw an astonishing light on the behaviour of the human brain under severe stress.

The purpose of abreaction is not, as once thought, to enable the patient to remember a suppressed event, but to cause him to blow off hitherto unexpressed emotion connected with an event which he may remember perfectly well. Various techniques were evolved by British and American doctors working with both servicemen and civilians, but among the most successful was the use of inhaled ether to make the patient as it were drunk and to release the strong control the patient had been unconsciously exerting; and then to induce these repressed emotions of fear, anger or panic, often by describing some quite fictitious event. The instance quoted by Dr W. Sargant is that of a tank soldier in whom abreaction was induced by persuading him, under ether intoxication, that he was trapped in a burning tank and had to fight his way out. This quite fictitious experience caused him to express and blow off the emotions of fear and panic which he had been suppressing, and whose suppression had been making him ill. Freud noted that reliving past events without any release of emotion had no therapeutic effect; and in fact the post-Freudian assumption that recalling forgotten incidents of the past will cure any mental illness is not even in accordance with Freud's teaching.

Abreaction is certainly no standard treatment of depression: severely depressed patients may be too deeply retarded to express emotion even under sedative drugs, and when they do, they tend to express the very depression for which a cure is being sought. But in early acute depressive reactions following extreme stress, such as wartime experiences, bereavement, kidnapping or hi-jacking, abreaction may have a place in releasing pent-up emotion.

Thirdly, there is leucotomy. This is an operation designed to separate off a small portion of the frontal lobe of the brain. This is the part of the brain that seems to be the seat of feelings of responsibility which, if overdeveloped, can become crippling obsessions. It was first used in 1936, but was based upon observations of accidental brain injuries going back many years. There are famous stories of soldiers being shot through the head and apparently none the worse for it; and the classical instance of an American railroad worker in the nineteenth century whose skull was totally transfixed by a steel bolt, but who had the bolt removed and lived on without physical disability.

In his case, however, and in that of many of the soldiers there was a marked change of personality, usually in the direction of irrresponsibility. They became selfish, emotionally shallow and unresponsive to other people's troubles and to the consequences of their own antisocial behaviour.

In the light of these many cases, and with increasingly precise knowledge of which part of the brain had been damaged, Moniz, a Portuguese neurologist and Nobel Prizewinner, began to operate on the frontal lobe in chronically ill (i.e. long-term) mental patients with remarkable results.

The main effect of leucotomy is to relieve tension, obsession and extreme worry, and even has a place in the treatment of intractable pain. After operation the patient still has the pain but is no longer worried by it. Even more, obsessional delusions may be relieved: a patient who has been in a mental hospital for years because he believes his appearance is so bizarre as to make normal life impossible, can face the world again and go back to work. He may still regard his appearance as bizarre but is no longer totally obsessed by it; and what is more, with the end of the obsessional reinforcement the belief itself may fade, so that the patient concludes he's a bit of a funny-looking chap but nothing out of the ordinary.

In early leucotomy, undesirable personality changes were a risk; patients tended to become more ordinary, less emotionally responsive. (But then it was their lack of ordinariness, their excessive responsiveness that made them ill in the first place.) With later modifications, the operation done through small burr-holes in the skull has become very much more precise, less of the frontal lobe is separated and the risk of undesirable changes has fallen to about 20 per cent.

It remains the treatment of last resort in depression, performed when all medical means including ECT have failed, where the patient remains severely incapacitated, where the risk of suicide is high and where the illness has been going on for a long time.

Skilfully performed on the right patient, it can restore a patient to a normal life and to his or her family and work. It is a better alternative than the lifetime of misery and incapacity that was the lot of the chronically depressed patient in the nineteenth century.

12

Suicide and arousal

It is the drama and disasters that get reported in medicine: both by the press, to whom good news is no news; and by doctors who tend to be writing from hospital where all the severe and desperate cases come. It is possible to spend a lifetime in general practice, treating depression among all the other illnesses that come one's way, and not have a single attempted suicide among one's depressed patients. Nevertheless it is always a chance and an unpredictable one; no patient is totally immune from the risk of suicide. Happily most depressed patients have good insight; they are aware that they are ill and that they need treatment, and many of them fear 'doing something silly'. So what follows should be read with this in mind, that suicide is relatively rare, and many badly depressed patients have felt themselves near suicide but made a full recovery without being drawn or driven to a serious attempt.

One or two popular misconceptions need to be dispelled. People say suicide is a cry for help, as if this somehow made it less dangerous. This may be so, or it may be a device to attract attention or to spite somebody close to the patient; but it may also be a serious attempt to die, and in any case it may succeed.

An even more dangerous generalisation is that people who threaten suicide never do it. Depressed patients don't bother to lie about suicide, and when such people feel themselves near to it they must invariably be taken seriously and given the most loving support. Hysterics will make wild announcements about impending doom; but in the course of a grand gesture they may well make an attempt which proves more successful than was intended.

I do not propose here to discuss the very difficult question of the hysteric; but when the depressed patient confesses to suicidal feelings, it is quite vital that he or she must *not* be rejected. 'What nonsense, pull yourself together, what a wicked thing to say after all we've done for you, when you have so much to live for'; any of these really wicked phrases could be a death sentence for a depressed patient. He has been rejected, dismissed, all help has been withdrawn; and above all his deep sense of guilt has been reinforced.

For there are two springs to suicide: on the one hand the patient may feel she can no longer face the misery in which she finds herself, the sheer pain of depression; and kills herself to escape from her symptoms. I have heard a patient already recovering well from one of her recurrent depressions say, 'I can't go through this again.' This is probably the commonest cause of suicide; and certainly this is so in the case of fatally ill or very old patients who decide rationally and responsibly on a dignified self-inflicted death.

On the other hand, the morbid sense of guilt may be so great as to drive the patient into a kind of self-execution. I have heard a patient say, 'How could anyone possibly go on being me?'; and where the sense of guilt is great this question takes on an awful urgency that admits of only one answer. It is possible that the more violent suicides, quite properly called self-destruction, spring from this cause.

I have spoken briefly and with sympathy of a dignified self-inflicted death. Suicide poses philosophical problems to the doctor in certain cases where it seems rational and sensible. As in most moral problems there is a gamut of response, from the terminal patient at one end who finds how well death serves the old and feeble, to the desperate teenager at the other end whose life, once saved, remains full of promise and of happiness. Nevertheless for practical purposes it is a doctor's job to treat all attempted suicides; in the vast majority of cases they are symptoms of illness, aberrations from which the patient can recover as surely and as permanently as from the apparently desperate symptoms of viral meningitis.

The best treatment of suicide is prevention, and the prevention of suicide must start early, before the desire to die becomes overwhelming. Nothing can prevent the determined suicide, except possibly an alert twenty-four-hour guard; but the patient can be drawn back from suicide by the attitude of loving acceptance I have already outlined; and in obscurer cases by an understanding of the phenomenon of arousal.

This is the word used by psychiatrists to describe what we might otherwise call stimulation, or response to stimulation. Many a depressed patient finds the ability to respond to outside demands, especially professional ones: so that a day's work that starts in lethargy and depression quite early takes on its own momentum, and the patient is able to function at his or her job almost free of the lassitude, retardation and guilt that seemed unsurmountable. One could express it, a little loosely, by saying he is pumping out adrenaline in response to the demand.

This is fine while the demand is there to be met: and this is certainly the mechanism by which people can stand great strain while the effort has to be made. But it is a very dangerous state to be in, because when the demand ceases, so do the effort and the adrenaline; and the patient may lapse into sudden and profound depression.

This is the case with the examples I have already quoted, the soldier who is all right in action and becomes ill on coming out of action; and the widow who copes magnificently until all the effort is over, and then collapses. And it is also probably the reason underlying what I have called the obscurer suicides, where someone may walk more or less straight from a successful meeting, a happy party or a great feat of survival, and take an overdose of sleeping pills.

The danger of arousal is thus: someone comes under excessive stress, starts perhaps to become depressed and in a misguided attempt to throw the whole thing off plunges into an orgy of work or pleasure or both. In this he is encouraged by the puritan/moral view of depression well expressed by Kipling in his 'Tale of the Camel's Hump'; and ill-informed well-intentioned people will urge him on to lose himself in his work. This is utterly wrong: the patient is imposing further stress on himself and making the illness worse when at last he has to stop; and then may come the sudden and totally unexpected suicide, either because the spell of work is over, or because the depression can finally no longer be fended off.

These tragedies can always be put in context *after* the event; but it takes a subtle mixture of skill, sympathy and authority to see the danger, and to check the patient in the course of overwork on which he is set. Anyone of the personality described in Chapter 2 subjected to a great emotion or other excessive stress, who tries to fight it with a frantic round of activity, needs a watchful (and slightly bossy) family, spouse or lover, and a good doctor in the background.

13

The scientific background

It is of course impossible to review nearly a hundred years of closely argued and largely conflicting research into depression in this one chapter. In fact the working doctor uses day to day only that small part of the world's research effort that he finds useful, practical and in accord with his experience.

He has learnt some in medical school and from his reading, some in exchange of clinical gossip with his colleagues, some from formal lectures and seminars, and a great deal from comparing all this, all these statements and opinions, with what he actually sees and hears in his practice.

Thus he will often find himself giving a firm clinical opinion, and being right at that, without being able to give chapter and verse of all the evidence and research upon which this opinion is founded; and many a humane and skilled doctor is treating depression thoroughly competently without giving a thought to either Pavlov or Freud.

These two researchers may be regarded as initiating and representing the two approaches to an 'explanation' of depression. The older is the psychodynamic, seeking to explain the derivation of these morbid emotions and perceptions from specific events; and often involving the concept of converted emotion. In this theory emotion that cannot be expressed for one reason or another is converted into another emotion that can find some expression, however unsatisfactory.

This is related to Freud's early hypothesis that the great

origin of anxiety (which is at least an expression of emotion, however unsatisfactory) is the transformation of unexpressed sexual energy: an idea that the world of the 1920s latched on to with undiscriminating glee.

Thus depression was described as retroflexed anger, where the desire to punish someone, something or the world as a whole was turned in on the patient's own self, resulting in the feeling of guilt, self-blame and self-destruction that we have seen.

Another psychodynamic theory suggested that the helplessness and hopelessness, the pessimism, hypochondria and retardation were learned from the patient's past, where experience of previous failures established a pattern of future failure in the patient's mind. This does not seem to me to take into account the number of depressed patients who have a better than average record in the past. In these patients depression seems more often the price of success than the result of failure.

A further theory is based on the way we learn from experience: over the years we acquire patterns of behaviour in accordance with the effect that behaviour has on our surroundings and fellow creatures. We learn to walk carefully on ice, to test the bath-water before we jump in, to look in the driving mirror before we pull out; and we learn to smile appropriately and say please and thank you. We learn which actions produce pleasant or useful results and which produce pain. If one form of behaviour is rewarded with a smile and one with a thick ear, we soon learn to prefer the former.

In the sort of situation I referred to in Chapter 3 as a period of frustrated emotion, in a boring job with unrewarding people, in a spell of anxiety where one cannot influence the outcome, in one's own or someone else's worrying illness, the behaviour we have come to rely upon as being beneficial is found not to work. Hard work goes for nothing, kindness and good manners are met with no response, one's own good intentions are not matched by other people or events.

This, as Pavlov originally demonstrated, leads to a confusion of behaviour: we abandon those beneficial activities we have laboriously learnt, and unconsciously experiment with new forms of behaviour to see if these work any better. Where these new forms also fail us, we become ill; where they work, we have found a way through to a different equilibrium.

This certainly *describes* certain forms of depression; but whether it offers much in the way of explanation I am more doubtful; and it has nothing useful to say about the depression following a sudden shock or trauma, where the disruption of behaviour and of thought may occur over a very short time indeed.

The other approach has been physiological and indeed biochemical; and the first systematic study of the physiology of the brain as an organ of the body comparable with the stomach or liver was undertaken by Pavlov in Russia in the first decade of this century.

Pavlov won the Nobel Prize in 1903 for research into the physiology of digestion. He had by then reached a stage where he felt he could get no further without investigating what he called the 'higher nervous activity' which seemed greatly to influence the digestion. This idea indeed was nothing new; the Woolf brothers in New York, investigating gastric ulcers in the 1860s, had shown how the state of the stomach lining varies with the mood of the patient (or the cat in certain cases). The concept of psychosomatic disease, that is to say somatic or bodily illness such as a stomach ulcer with an emotional background, was well established in conventional physiology quite early in this century.

Pavlov is best known for his investigation of the conditioned reflex: but in fact his most valuable research was into subtler reactions of the brain, including the implantation of neuroses and their subsequent relief. Unhappily his work has provided the basis for the most effective forms of brain washing and political indoctrination, as the Soviet government was quick to recognise: though a passionate and outspoken opponent of the régime all his life, Pavlov was generously supported by Russian governments from Lenin on.

However, his work equally provided a rational approach to the treatment of battle neuroses in the Second World War. Doctors were puzzled by the paradoxical behaviour of patients admitted from the blitz and battlefields in conditions like shellshock; and found in translations of Pavlov's last lectures on *Conditioned Reflexes and Psychiatry* close parallels between this behaviour and that of Pavlov's dogs in which 'experimental neuroses' had been induced.

He had demonstrated in a series of carefully controlled experiments that dogs' behaviour can be altered predictably by various stresses; and had repeated these experiments over and over again until he was able to establish with certainty how the brain responds to various stimuli. Many of his experiments make distressing reading for a modern audience but his results were clear, testable and useful in psychiatry.

Moreover, they increasingly ran parallel with other laboratory work in brain physiology; and above all it became established that the brain as an organ has a physiological response as predictable as that of the stomach or liver, though of course over a much wider scope. And once the concept had been grasped that behaviour is a function of the brain, and the brain is an organ capable of ordinary physiological investigation, the way was open to a much clearer understanding of certain types of abnormal behaviour.

The biochemistry of the brain was investigated firstly by the examination of dead brains. The analysis of the brains of suicides, for instance, in the 1960s showed among other things a consistent decrease in 5-hydroxytryptamine (5-HT), an important substance in the transmission of nerve impulses, and its metabolites; and later investigations among depressed and normal subjects confirmed (1) that 5-HT is decreased in the bloodstream of depressed patients; and (2) that such people have impaired ability to transport 5-HT in the blood even when they are not depressed.

The thyroid and its reaction on and in depression has also been extensively studied, as have sodium levels in the cerebrospinal fluid (examined by lumbar puncture) and these and many other biochemical examinations over the last twenty-five years have shown that depression is certainly *accompanied* by a wide range of chemical changes, though whether these changes *cause* or *are* the illness is a matter of philosophy.

It is certain from this that biochemical changes in the brain, in the cerebrospinal fluid and in the bloodstream occur in depression; that these changes are modified or reversed by physical and chemical antidepressant treatment; and that as these biochemical levels return towards normal, the symptoms improve. This is the basis for the claim that depression is, as Freud once hinted, a biochemical illness; and this is why the biochemical treatment of depression is rational and effective.

14

Depression at work

It is often important that members of management, staff or work force should know something about depression; firstly because it enables them all to be more sympathetic to colleagues, superiors and juniors who are suffering this illness; and secondly because the illness is sometimes a reason for behaviour that would otherwise appear inexplicable. What is more, the skilled and sympathetic senior person may be able to spot warning signs in the people he or she is responsible for, possibly avert trouble, and very likely get the patient to treatment quicker if trouble does occur.

All diagnosis depends on change: what everybody does or looks like every day we call normal; so anybody whose behaviour alters from the usual pattern needs a sympathetic alertness from those around.

Probably the first sign in any chronic illness is deterioration in work: typing mistakes, errors in figures, poor time-keeping, bad quality craft work, slowness. None of these means depression in itself but any may mean illness, including alcoholism.

A change of personality is often subtler and more insidious; one realises after a variable amount of time that the sunny and willing has become morose and unhelpful; the out-going and gregarious has become withdrawn; the resolute and reliable has become forgetful, indecisive, tearful.

Anyone can be upset for a while; but such behaviour prolonged over a week or two is unlikely to be sulks, disappointment, even quite long-term worry. We have practised psychological mechanisms for absorbing adverse circumstances *and* going on living; and total failure to adapt reasonably is probably morbid.

At work, reactions are partly determined by the patient's position. Tears, whether stormy or resigned, are just not available to a macho young lorry-driver, a steady artisan of 50 or a managing director of any age. In such men irritability, aggressiveness, or bad temper are more likely expressions of early distress; while sulks and tears are, if feminists will forgive the observation, more likely in a young woman in a junior position.

In a similar way, indecisiveness, a cardinal symptom of depression may be totally overlooked in a typist or a junior accountant; but it shows up very markedly in a senior executive, and in fact one not infrequently hears junior executives complain they cannot 'get a decision' out of their boss. Again, junior members of staff have learnt to hide the grumpiness or irritability that may indicate the early paranoia of depression; while more senior and self-indulgent members of the hierarchy may give theirs full rein.

A more serious depression is no respecter of rank and person, and the observed symptoms become much more similar. Lack of concentration and forgetfulness are as noticeable in an office boy, a boiler man or a messenger as in a chief engineer, though the effect *may* be less serious; and only the very insensitive and unobservant could miss the silent withdrawn patient, the subdued manner and appearance, the general sense that a light has been turned down, the personality darkened.

Certain textbooks make great play of appearance in depression; and certainly if someone who is normally well turned out becomes consistently shabby and slovenly something is wrong. Many depressed patients preserve a perfectly trim external appearance, but where these changes do occur, they may leave the sympathetic observer to think more closely about that person's behaviour and performance over the last few weeks.

Some symptoms may seem bizarre. Panic attacks may seem to the observer a bit of hysterical play-acting, and when they cause the patient to rush from the room this is even more puzzling. Even without panic attacks, depressed patients have difficulty in facing people, and they have to go to enormous lengths to avoid confronting their boss (or indeed their junior), people with whom they have business, and anybody outside their immediate familiar circle. It may appear as a sudden access of paralysing shyness.

Sometimes in a depression the patient finds it almost impossible to speak at all, and cannot really even answer straight questions. People cannot face the office, or alternatively cannot leave their own office, or panic in the lavatory and cannot come out.

Paranoia may be quite severe, and the patient may complain of a colleague's harassment, non-co-operation or other unreasonable or unfair treatment; and this can lead to a lot of time wasted in enquiry and a lot of ill-feeling before the true nature of the complaint is sorted out. The paranoia may indeed be so severe as to lead to a suspicion of schizophrenia, always an alarming diagnosis on all sides.

Attention having been aroused, what can boss or colleague do? I suggest he or she should keep it simple, keep it direct. Do not ask, 'Are you worrying about anything? Is anything wrong?': this puts a burden of explanation on the patient, in a way it puts him in the wrong and increases both the guilt of the illness and its other side, the resentment the patient feels at not being understood.

It is better to ask the straight question 'How are you? How do you feel?' The patient will probably give some evasive reply such as, 'Oh, all right,' and the questioner might reasonably persist on the lines, 'You don't seem at all yourself recently, I thought you might be feeling out of sorts.'

If this gets nowhere, and it very well may not as the patient's shame, guilt and indeed bewilderment at the illness erect huge barriers of concealment, I think it is legitimate for some senior person to insist, so far as anybody has any right to insist, that the patient should see a doctor; and even, at the risk of being thought an interfering pompous ass by the doctor, write *by post* to the doctor describing the changes that have been observed in the patient's behaviour, performance and appearance. *Don't* suggest a diagnosis: we doctors are a touchy lot.

Just how far this process of kindly pressure can go depends on two factors: on the one hand the personality of the firm, how paternalistic, how informal, how friendly it is; and on the personality of both boss and patient, how well they know each other, how much each respects and trusts the other and so on. On the other hand the patient's job may be an important factor: if it involves big decisions, large sums of money, important representation of the firm to the outside world or even actual physical danger to colleagues or the general public, the office will be much more anxious to order the patient home, not to return without a medical certificate. This is a tough procedure but one has to concede to companies a degree of legitimate concern over employees' competence. Whether this is handled in the patient's department or wholly by the personnel department is a matter of company procedure, and above all of the personalities involved.

In fact, most depressed patients, despite their concealment and their probably wrong-headed determination to remain at work, have fairly good insight into their condition: they know they are ill. They probably have particular friends at work who can help and act as confidants, especially by softening somewhat the hard edge of obstinacy which is what drives many depressives into depression.

One must guard against adding to the patient's burden and existing guilt the shame and failure of being sent home from work: but it may be an enormous relief to admit the illness and have at least one decision taken by somebody else. Tact and kindness will soften the blow, one hopes: after all the patient has in effect been wounded in action; and with the doctor's help he or she may be back at work long before expected, if not completely well at least coping, with self-respect restored, and saved by the vigilance of colleagues from a worse and longer illness.

15

Depression in history

We live in an age in some ways curiously without roots. Whether we are inclined to think ourselves unique, or whether other ages have equally failed to keep up with their past, there has certainly been an extraordinary tendency during the last twenty years or so to speak and write as if all modern phenomena were unprecedented, and as if nobody had ever had our troubles before. This is largely untrue; and it is certainly quite untrue to think that depression is a unique and modern illness. It is true that we have got better at recognising it: in my own professional lifetime certain symptoms which used to be thought anxiety or schizophrenic have been recognised as depressive; and of course with more satisfactory treatment the illness becomes more easily recognised. Heaven knows how many sufferers in the past from the vapours, megrims, a decline, fading away, melancholy or reclusiveness might have been helped by antidepressants; and it is sometimes possible to pick out the depressive picture through the mist of imagery and loose vocabulary.

Melancholy and melancholia figure largely in literature, and carry a wide range of different meanings: from Milton's 'divinest melancholy', the comfortable and romantic musings of a literary gent, to Robert Burton's enormously long description of the state in 1621, in many ways an astonishingly modern work to which we shall return. Keats wrote his 'Ode to Melancholy', even more than Milton's a work of romantic reverie, and I do not think he was a depressive. Lamb, who was, wrote an 'Essay on Melancholy', so one has to be careful of the word.

72

Madness is another word not to be relied upon. It is in any case not a medical term but a legal, social or even political one, implying behaviour, perceptions or indeed opinions so far at variance with those of your fellow-citizens, that they decide they can no longer be doing with you, and put you away; and all psychiatrists are to a greater or lesser extent haunted with a concept of normality wished upon them by society. We can see the political use of this in the Soviet Union, and sometimes, by error I trust, in our own society.

Frequently in the past the error was clinical: patients, for instance, with severe underactivity of the thyroid in which psychosis and dementia may be features have been shut up in asylums; and fairly recent research has shown that poor mad George III suffered from a metabolic illness called porphyria.

There is a danger when riding one's hobby-horse that one may select from the contemporary evidences just the bit one wants, and go depression-hunting through history and literature in a quite irresponsible fashion; but all I would like to show here is that depression is no new thing, and we are quite wrong to think it is. Ruskin and Schumann, for instance, both of whom are described as subjects of fits of madness, were pretty clearly depressive, and Ruskin probably manic-depressive. Dr Johnson was famous for his depressions. He either worked in manic bursts or could not bring himself to work at all, full of guilt and self-blame; like many another student, he seriously thought of suicide before he left Oxford; and all his life was marked by periods of intense depression and withdrawal, with a deep sense of sin and prayers to God for improvement.

The evidence is better from about the mid-eighteenth century on, when biography became more popular, because it is easier to find depression in literature than in history. Depressed patients do not make history. They retreat into monasteries like the Emperor Charles V, or retire from their art and become recluses like Duparc; history is full of active, reasonably successful men and women who suddenly disappear until their death is recorded thirty years later: and it is tempting to see untreated depression in some at least of these.

In the Old Testament, Chapter 16 of the first book of Samuel, verse 23 reads: 'And it came to pass, when the evil spirit from God was upon Saul, that David took an harp, and played with his hand: so Saul was refreshed, and was well, and the evil spirit departed from him.' Many a later patient has found music a relief in a minor depression, and this sounds very like the earliest reference to depression. It is not too fanciful to see a depressive pattern in some of the spectacular griefs and sulks in the *Iliad*.

By far the fullest and most valuable evidence that depression is no new thing is contained in *The Anatomy of Melancholy* by Robert Burton, a vastly erudite, enormously leisured gallimaufry of learning, anecdote, superstition, observation and robust common sense that meanders for some thousand pages of modern small print reviewing the whole subject of depression and melancholia from angles social, religious, moral, sexual and quasi-anatomical till the reader's head spins. His anatomy concerns itself with humors, spirits, black bile, gall and choler; his treatment include wine of hellebore, spirit of borage, diambra, dianthus, conserve of violets, treacle, mithridate, polypody and pennyroyal. But among possible causes he lists a blow on the head, preceding disease, overmuch study, vehement labour, and passions and perturbations, all of which can be fitted into the modern hypothalamic view of depression.

What particularly strikes one as modern in his approach is his resolutely and comfortingly rational approach in an age little removed from mediaeval superstition: 'To give some satisfaction to melancholy men that are troubled with these symptoms, a better mean in my judgment cannot be taken, than to show them the cause whence they proceed; not from devils as they suppose, or that they are bewitched or forsaken of God.' No wonder Sir William Osler called it the greatest medical treatise written by a layman. This is the greatest message of comfort the modern doctor can bring to the depressed patient, and Robert Burton had already got it in the seventeenth century.

(In fact this may not have been so great a personal achievement; the treatment of melancholia and similar 'mental' illnesses at that time was largely organic and chemical, though the chemicals were all derived from herbs: it is poppy and mandragora that Iago mentions in jeering at Othello. This was before nineteenth-century psychological theory separated mind and body into two compartments: a separation possibly increased initially as modern physiology learnt more about the brain without at that time necessarily learning more about the mind.)

The other great source of contemporary views of melancholy and depression is Shakespeare. One finds references to melancholy scattered throughout his works, and usually in the context of a genuine depression rather than Keats's and Milton's romantic indulgence: which indeed is not wholly absent from Robert Burton. Shakespeare's green and yellow melancholy is associated with grief and bereavement; and in *The Merchant of Venice* Antonio opens the play with the words, 'In sooth, I know not why I am so sad', the classic comment of the depressed patient. 'It wearies me;' he goes on, 'you say it wearies you; But how I caught it, found it, or came by it, . . . I am to learn. And such a want-wit sadness makes of me, That I have much ado to know myself.'

One could hardly look for a better description of the depressed frame of mind; and in the exchanges that follow Antonio's friends, as kind friends will, offer explanations or causes for his depression, or diversions to take his mind off it, while Antonio stands practically silent, rejecting the explanations and ignoring the diversions. It is in this state that Bassanio finds him and begs him for a loan to court Portia; and it is in this state that he accepts Shylock's disastrous bond. It is true Antonio shows an unlikely optimism about his ships at sea; but of his sadness and taciturnity Shakespeare leaves us in no doubt.

Melancholy in the romantic sentimental sense there is in plenty, in *Twelfth Night, As You Like It, All's Well That Ends Well* and even in Cleopatra, that superb clinical picture of hysteria. But Shakespeare's greatest portrayal of depression is in *Hamlet*. In Hamlet's lines one finds the guilt and self-blame of the depressed, the indecisiveness, suicidal thoughts and motives, paranoia and sleep disturbance, too many refrences to quote. Consider only the speeches beginning, 'O! that this too too solid flesh would melt'; O! what a rogue and peasant slave am I'; 'To be or not to be'; 'Now might I do it pat, now he is praying'; and 'How all occasions do inform against me', for the guilt, violent self-blame and suicidal feelings.

Other characters describe his sad looks and dark dress, beyond common mourning for his father; Ophelia tells of 'a sigh so piteous and profound That it did seem to shatter all his bulk'; and the unfortunate and indistinguishable Rosencrantz and Guildenstern are set to their spying with a description of Hamlet's near madness.

I do not myself think Shakespeare was a depressive. There are details in *Hamlet* that do not sufficiently fit the typical picture. One must allow for artistic licence and exigencies of the plot and action; and Hamlet's hysterical behaviour after meeting the ghost could be regarded as the up-swing of a manic-depressive personality. But his behaviour with Ophelia and Polonius looks more like conventional Elizabethan madness, often hardly to be distinguished from foolery; and I feel in general the character is drawn from observation, like Cleopatra's hysteria, rather than precise personal experience. But that observation is so clear and recognisable that no one could possibly think depression a uniquely modern illness.

16

Case histories

In academic medical circles, what is called 'anecdotal' evidence is regarded with scorn. There is no statistical basis to interesting sidelines in medicine, and it is certainly true that one must not base a generalisation or a wide opinion on one or two cases. All the same, case histories flesh out the bones of medical theory, and I make no apology for offering a series of medical anecdotes; it will help depressed patients to feel less separated and alone if they hear a few stories of fellow-suffers.

It is an important common feature of these stories that no prolonged psychological history is needed to understand them. It has to be emphasised over and over again that these depressions are illnesses like pneumonia; they are recognised by their group of symptoms, which are remarkably specific and uniform. The more I see of depression the more precise my criteria of diagnosis become; and on those occasions when I have thought this is probably depression, or this would do for depression, I have been wrong.

Case I: We can start with a very typical story. This was a girl of 24, normally attractive and lively, doing a good job in a busy office, living with a young man who was working for professional qualifications. Both sets of parents had discountenanced marriage before he was qualified.

She was depressed, she said, for no reason; she tended to go up and down, two or three weeks down, several weeks up; in the up weeks she was giggly and rather high. In the down spells, which were taking over, she felt she could not face the office. She had a constant sense of missing out from something but did not know what. She was physically lethargic, getting to sleep late and waking late; and felt guiltily that she was not doing her work properly. She was off sex in the down spells.

Treatment was started with one of the tricyclic antidepressants, and in about three weeks she reported an increase in energy, though getting more tired because she was doing more. Although she had previously said the depression was no worse before her periods, she now found she was in fact less 'ratty' before a period. She was dreaming a lot, what she called 'very active dreams'.

A fortnight later she reported an attack of depersonalisation and panic at work the previous day. She was having rather more difficulty getting to sleep, the very active dreams had changed to nightmares, and she was waking drugged. The treatment was changed to a different tricyclic; and three weeks later she reported an immediate change in the sleep pattern, getting off to sleep better, waking fresher, able to face the morning and the crowded tube.

She had fewer down days; she was getting through a lot of work. She said she was getting very tired, having a good rest at the weekend, and then getting over it. She was getting worse side-effects from the tablets, a very dry mouth, sweating a lot, constipated and a poor appetite. She was still off sex.

During the next month she had a bad week or ten days with bad sleep and early waking; she was finding work an effort again, and was finding her colleagues irritating. The tablets were increased, and at the next visit she had made great strides. This was six or seven weeks from starting treatment.

Although sleep was still not too good, she was working hard and effectively, getting through a lot and not getting very tired. Above all, she said, 'I've fallen in love all over again.'

She kept up her improvement on a maintenance dose of tricyclics. Her boyfriend qualified, and they married about nine months from starting treatment. She was off tablets after

Case histories

a year, took them briefly again about eighteen months from the original treatment, and then successfully tapered them off over the next few weeks. She remained well.

It is typical of many depressives that she most consistently related her clinical improvement to work performance: she seemed throughout more concerned with how she was doing her job than how she felt, which is characteristic of the depressive's conscientiousness. In her case it was very hard to find the event that triggered off the depression, and for practical purposes it really did not matter.

Case II: The next patient, aged 29, who actually worked for the same firm, showed exactly the same conscientious and hard-working temperament but presented very different symptoms. She had been feeling sick on and off for two or three years, with no appetite and loss of weight. She said she felt she was not doing her job correctly, and was worrying over this; she might burst into tears if anyone reproved her, which was wholly out of character.

The phrase 'on and off' led to enquiry about each particular episode: each stated with an excess of lethargy, both physical and mental. She would lose her appetite, smoke more and get a dry mouth. She slept well but got nocturnal diarrhoea in these episodes.

She was depressed at times and a bit paranoid, feeling people were looking at her oddly or critically. There was a fair amount of self-blame, feeling she was letting everybody down. Memory and decision-making remained but she could not keep her concentration if faced by a volume of work. She took a pessimistic view of her circumstances, family health and holiday prospects, and she showed some typical obsessional rumination, worrying over small things that had gone wrong.

Her job was in fact something of a worry. She was a senior computer programmer or analyst, writing instructions for programming branch computers. It emerged in the next few weeks that her first job at head office had been too easy for her, she had become bored and perhaps a bit complacent, and she had reckoned to learn her new senior job as she went along. There proved to be a huge amount to learn and a good deal of management, and she was unreasonably cast down by small failures.

The abdominal symptoms left the doctor uneasy about a simple diagnosis; but he started her on a small and increasing dose of antidepressants while considering and investigating the nausea and diarrhoea. About three weeks later the patient reported fainting at the office while feeling severely nauseated. She was very tired and lacking in energy, forcing herself to stay awake and sleeping 20 hours a day at the week-end. She also had a mild cystitis.

A fortnight later, when the dose had increased, there was a big improvement; in particular she was sleeping almost normally and eating well. It was at this point that she was able to talk about the job problems and the excessive stress they were generating.

By the eighth week of treatment she said she was feeling fine; she still felt bloated and a bit sick after too big a meal but otherwise could eat whatever she liked and enjoy it. Her office, who were very sympathetic, had given her an easier job, and though she was quite happy with it, it now seemed insufficient challenge, and she wanted more to do. On the other hand, her boss could still reduce her to tears, usually to his intense embarrassment and remorse.

Improvement was maintained over the next six weeks or so, during which not only did she have builders in her flat but the Christmas holiday came with all its traumas and anxieties. She made no particular report about dreaming this time but she did say that she had woken two or three times soaked in sweat. Nevertheless she said she had not felt so relaxed for years; she had done a public speaking course and managed very well; and she had taken a stranger out to a business lunch without either tension or nausea. She was taking on more responsibility at work.

Early in January she had one of the down-swings which almost always characterise recovery from depression: she started waking at frequent intervals during the night, often soaked in sweat and probably after nightmares. She had lost her appetite again, and the nausea and dirrhoea had recurred.

This coincided with a change in her job specification, which she was to try for three months under supervision. She was not happy about this, and it can be seen as an increase in stress in a patient beginning to recover from previous excessive stress. Ups and downs occur in recovery often for no very good reason, but here the coincidences were very close: a month later she took what she described as a horrendous decision to give up all management responsibilities, and concentrate on the purely technical side of her work. She said she was very disappointed but greatly relieved, and began to sleep well again from the moment the decision was accepted by her office.

A month later she said she was a different girl; all the symptoms had cleared, and her nausea and diarrhoea were things of the past. She was taking on certain managerial functions despite her decision, and was coping well. She tapered off all treatment seven or eight months from starting.

I think this history illustrates two particular points: firstly the diagnosis of depression is not always as easy as perhaps I make it seem, and may be bedevilled with physical symptoms that need attention and investigation while the doctor is also looking into the depression.

Secondly, depression is a stress illness, and ideally needs release from the particular stress that is triggering it. As suggested earlier, this is not always possible, but the change in this patient when she had taken this important decision was remarkable. Of course she was probably incapable of taking this decision until the illness was well under treatment.

Case III: This was a 15-year-old schoolboy. I had already treated his grandfather, father and elder brother for depression, and when he first came to me, I thought he was repeating the family pattern. He had been tired, dopey and depressed for about three months, and feeling at his worst in the evening. His memory was a bit worse than usual and his concentration was not very good, but decision-making was unimpaired. He was uncommunicative and withdrawn, and finding school work very difficult; he found games totally exhausting. He was sleeping normally when first seen, and there was at no time any sense of guilt or self-blame.

He had had headaches all this time, getting more frequent, more severe and long lasting as time went on. This is rare in depression. He also looked ill in a way different from most depressed patients: it is true that many such patients suddenly look years younger towards the end of treatment, but they do not often look obviously physically ill when first seen. It seemed unlike a straightforward depression.

He came from a part of Scotland where brucellosis was particularly common; this is a disease of cattle and sheep rather like glandular fever, often acquired by humans either through milk or by working closely with the creatures as this boy had been doing. In this case the infection could not be proved; various doctors were involved because the boy was travelling between Scotland and England, and various treatments were tried. Antidepressants spectacularly failed to help, and the symptoms only got better when treatment for brucellosis was given despite the lack of proof.

This patient developed a classical reactive depression five years later, which responded well to antidepressants. The striking difference in management between these two illnesses shows that some depressions are directly and solely caused by another illness such as glandular fever, malaria or flu, and recover as the underlying illness gets better. In the case of long-running illnesses like brucellosis, this can be a great difficulty for the doctor.

Case IV: This was a 30-year-old research assistant, always he said a tense and worrying sort of man, but whose tension had recently greatly increased in a period of extra stress at work. The occasion of his coming to see me was an episode when he had felt so tense at a meeting that he had had to rush out, hurry home and burst into tears.

He had been fairly depressed for some time, and after this all self-confidence deserted him. He was still depressed, at the sullen and withdrawn level, with no real variation from one part of the day to another. There was no real change in sleep pattern, though he had two or three nights a month of difficulty getting off, staying awake till about two thirty in the morning.

He had quite a high-pressure job which was going pretty well, and he was coping with it satisfactorily. His memory was entirely adequate, and his concentration and decision-making were as good as ever. When I asked him, 'At your worst, do you find yourself blaming other people, life with a capital L or yourself?' He replied mainly other people; but he blamed himself somewhat and Life somewhat.

He was physically below par but he was working very hard and was short of exercise; he had increased his smoking to twenty-five cigarettes a day. There was no real physical symptom beyond some looseness of the bowels the first two days of each week, almost certainly an anxiety symptom at the start of each week's work.

I concluded that this was not depression. Despite his tension he was coping at work and intellectual retardation was absent, this is to say memory, concentration and decision-making were all more or less normal. There was no serious disturbance of sleep, and there was little self-blame. All these are important diagnostic features of depression, and I would hesitate to diagnose the illness if they are absent.

This was an anxiety state, to which the patient was clearly

prone, and which can at times be confused with depression. It improved with a little mild sedation, much discussion, a little advice and above all an improvement in his work pressures.

Case V: This 21-year-old girl presented with a sort of two-pronged history: on the one hand she had had an unusual number of colds and particularly of sore throats in the past year or more; on the other hand she seemed to have a mild but pretty classical depression. However, as the depression was enquired into many details were not quite right for the classical picture. Ture, there was considerable loss of memory, of concentration and of decision-making; and she said she was less enthusiastic and cheerful than usual. Sleep pattern was certainly disturbed; sometimes she slept well, and sometimes woke at midnight or one o'clock in the morning; she would then doze or read a bit, get off to sleep again, and wake with difficulty, heavy and dopey in the morning. She did not feel normally sexy.

On the other hand she felt fed-up rather than genuinely depressed, and though she felt guilty, this was *because* she was feeling fed-up. She was rather more easily upset than usual, jumpy and nervous, and particularly nervous of being out socially; but her nerves and jumpiness never amounted to panic. Part of her avoidance of social contacts was just because she was tired. There was several physical symptoms; and while physical symptoms certainly occur in depression, these were not at all typical. There were the sore throats; there were frequent coughs; she had little or no appetite; she was feeling the cold more than usual.

All these atypical elements left her doctor uneasy about the diagnosis, particularly as she also had a very small swelling of the thyroid gland: again not at all uncommon and often of no significance, but raising doubts in this case.

Blood tests did indeed show an abnormal thyroid function, of a slightly unusual sort, and she made a full recovery, including all the depressive symptoms, on thyroid treatment.

Case VI: No serious-minded person need read this next section: the patient was a parrot, confusingly called Turkey. Turkey lived in a large and lively household where he (or possibly she) was much visited and conversed with. For some reason which no one could later remember, his cage was moved to a very quiet part of the house where no one went at all frequently except to clean his cage.

Turkey became ill. He ceased to whistle and talk, he became immobile, sitting hunched in one corner of his cage, and he took no notice of the few people who did visit him. He lost his appetite. A member of the family, with my connivance, diagnosed depression, and the cage was moved back to its more frequented position. Gradually over the next three or four days, Turkey recovered. He became more mobile, first responding to people just by moving his head; then he began to shuffle about his perch a bit. He ate a little; he whistled once or twice. By the fourth day he was his usual self, whistling though not yet talking, flying about his cage, puffed up and well groomed, a renewed delight to the family.

Now, I cannot swear that Turkey had a depression. He *may* have been suffering agonies of guilt and self-blame but one cannot be sure. He was certainly retarded, and may have had a diminished memory during this time. But in Pavlovian terms (see Chapter 13) he did throw an interesting light on such human phenomena as sensory deprivation, which is widely used as a torture in our enlightened century, and which used to be a complication of cataract operations in elderly people who used to be nursed blindfold and immobile after the operation; and such as depression in isolated old people, in whom one can say either that the lack of stimulation is a stress, or that actual *lack* of stress is causing a depression.

At all events, in this tale of human distress and human interest, I feel Turkey has earned a place.

17

Conclusion

I suggested at the beginning of this book that what one might call the ordinary-ignorant approach to depression is much bedevilled by what are really philosophical considerations; and here at the end of the discussion we should consider some of these philosophical aspects of depression which are interesting and even important.

I have emphasised all along that the dreadful feelings of guilt, failure and impending doom are merely symptoms. Nevertheless they are very real to the patient, and strike deep into her essence and personality. Guilt, laziness and lethargy are all foreign to the depressive personality, and here she is, deep sunk in all three. The artist loses talent, and can no longer appreciate colour; the religious man loses his faith in God, no longer knows God or is convinced of God's anger; the normally charitable are aware of a failure of love towards their fellow men.

All these and many other deeply moral feelings lie heavily on the depressed patient, and present the doctor with an equal moral ambiguity in apparently offering to cure such sins with a pill. Such an approach seems at times to belittle the patient, floundering as he is in a tragic sea of failure, self-doubt and self-disgust; and while the assurance that this is illness, not sin or failure, may bring immense relief, sin and failure are bruises that need handling as gently as any bodily injury.

There is a theology of depression. I mentioned earlier 'there is nothing new, and nothing true, and nothing matters':

and this is a fair definition of the mediaeval sin of accidie, which we have translated as sloth. A mediaeval writer pointed out that a patient with jaundice will think the whole world yellow, and lose his faith in God; and to offer a pill apparently for sin must seem to the patient a fearful responsibility and, indeed, impertinence for the doctor to undertake.

All this takes gentle handling. I have mentioned the young woman who blamed herself for the death of her little boy: it was quite impossible at a first meeting to say in effect 'I will give you a pill to take away the blame'; it took three meetings before I could effectively suggest treatment. I think there is no substitute for gradually convincing the patient of the usefulness and indeed correctness of this rather hard-boiled physiological approach I have been presenting. I generally get him or her to concentrate on the most obvious physical, mood and intellectual symptoms, the bad sleep, bad memory, tiredness, and so on; and suggest that the grave and unresolvable philosophical doubts may be left until later. Such patients, being particularly tough-minded, do particularly well as a rule.

In a more humanist context there are those, including some doctors, who argue that the patient is simply unhappy, and what use on earth are pills to him? This is like the problem-they-can't-cope-with, pull-yourself-together school of thought: it manages to be both unscientific and inhumane at the same time. The motive no doubt is respectable: the speaker recognises unhappiness as a human reality, and feels that we should all take responsibility for any situation we find ourselves in. There is also an element of fashionable medical nihilism about it: the reaction against the over-enthusiasm for wonder drugs is an equally unbalanced belief that all medicines are wrong, and that doctors shouldn't really *do* anything to help anybody.

It is unscientific because to say depression is only unhappiness is exactly comparable to saying that appendicitis is only stomach ache. So it is: the trick is to tell one stomach ache from another: it is called diagnosis and it is highly spoken of.

It is inhumane because it puts the speaker's beliefs and convictions above the patient's welfare. The medical nihilism I have mentioned emerges from a peculiar flight from reason over the last twenty-five years. Fringe sects, strange beliefs, weird diets and weirder cults, many coming from the East and most ending in California, demand complicated approaches to illness. For people in this frame of mind nothing will serve that is not tortuous, mystic and arcane; the physiological view of depression is just too simple, 'There must be more to it than that,' they say.

But this way patients get better; and while the doctor must acknowledge the moral thin ice over which he or she is stepping, the patient's welfare requires a coherent and repeatable scheme of diagnosis and treatment which gives intelligible support; effective improvement and rational hope.